PENGUIN BOOKS

THE ADVENTURES OF SPEEDFALL

John Fuller was born in 1937 and is a Fellow of Magdalen College, Oxford. He has published nine collections of poems, from which there is a generous selection in his *Selected Poems 1954–1982*, published in Penguin. Some of his poetry for children appears in *Poets in Hand: A Puffin Quintet*. His first work of adult fiction, *Flying to Nowhere* (1983) won the Whitbread Literary Award for the Best First Novel in that year and was short-listed for the Booker McConnell Prize. He is married, with three daughters, and divides his time between Oxford and his Cottage in North Wales.

JOHN FULLER

THE ADVENTURES OF SPEEDFALL

PENGUIN BOOKS

Penguin Books Ltd, Harmondsworth, Middlesex, England
Viking Penguin Inc., 40 West 23rd Street, New York, New York 10010, U.S.A.
Penguin Books Australia Ltd, Ringwood, Victoria, Australia
Penguin Books Canada Limited, 2801 John Street, Markham, Ontario, Canada L3R 1B4
Penguin Books (N.Z.) Ltd, 182–190 Wairau Road, Auckland 10, New Zealand

First published by The Salamander Press 1985
Published in Penguin Books 1986

Printed and bound in Great Britain by
Cox & Wyman Ltd, Reading

For Nicky, Nick and the Red Nun

ACKNOWLEDGMENT

Some of these stories first appeared in the *Listener*, the *New Review* and the *Poetry Review*.

CONTENTS

Wriggly Porridge

You will remember that brief period in our constitutional history when both the Prime Minister and the Leader of the Opposition were old members of St Patrick's College, Oxford. Perhaps you may be forgiven for never having noticed such a recondite coincidence. You certainly would not have known of the terrible danger that threatened the world at the time, a danger originating in neither of the right honourable gentlemen's policies, irresponsible as they were, but in what Speedfall always referred to as wriggly porridge.

In fact, the whole thing was Speedfall's fault. I heard the inside story from him when I suppose he thought the danger was over, and there could be no harm in turning it into a sensational anecdote. I advised him to keep quiet about it. It wasn't the sort of episode you could safely call terminated. There might have been a number of awkward questions asked.

But Speedfall isn't, I'm afraid, at all the sort of chap to feel chastened and subdued.

You must first understand how, in a mysterious way unique among human organisations, the Governing Body of an Oxford College can be at once profoundly aware of the need for some particular course of action and profoundly unable to do anything about it. Indeed, the more unnecessary the policy the better, as far as this paradox is concerned, for then a College will be all the more convinced of its efficacy and all the more incapable of putting it into effect.

At that time, St Patrick's knew very well that it should hold an election to an Honorary Fellowship, there being such a vacancy on the foundation. Once the subject had been raised, it was taken as self-evident that the whole edifice of religion, education and scholarship would be rapidly ruined if the vacancy were not filled. The usual impasse was in this case reached quickly. The preferred candidate was the Leader of the Opposition, a Tory of the old school, with impeccable vowels; but as the Fellowship Committee's memorandum scrupulously observed, the College could not in this case reveal its political bias by electing *only* the Leader of the Opposition. It would have to elect the Prime Minister as well. But this was impossible for two reasons: first, the pair would be at each other's throats and turn every College feast into a bear garden (or worse still, would simply not come, making a mockery of the honour); second, there was no provision in the statutes for electing more than the stated number of Honorary Fellows.

The Fellowship Committee put the matter back into the hands of the Governing Body, thus preparing the way for Speedfall and his wriggly porridge.

Speedfall in any case was the soul of indiscretion. Even his freshmen, shut in the unfallen Bastille of Introductory Logic, were sustained by the bread-and-water of his topical syllogisms ('No member of the Labour Party possesses a shooting-stick' was how one began, I seem to remember, and went on to imply that most Fellows of St Patrick's were snobs). It wasn't long before the whole College could talk of nothing else.

There were other names mentioned. One group of older Fellows had proposed a hanging judge of such senility and conservatism that even the Principal had not taken him seriously for a moment, himself preferring a Finnish lexicographer of unparalleled obscurity. Gestures like these, half-hearted as they were, merely underlined the basic impossibility of the situation. The tentative rehearsal of other names, all distinguished men in their fields, did nothing to suggest a solution.

But fools rush in where angels fear to tread. Or rather, Speedfall rushes in where angels fear to tread, for Speedfall has the disarmingly unconceited conviction that clear thinking is the only passport to choice and decision, and that only a training in philosophy leads to really clear thinking. He wouldn't, if pressed, have claimed an absolute monopoly in discrimination and decisiveness, but he was never thus pressed. Who could believe it of a man for whom, wondering if he should visit his sick aunt, the crucial point of interest, pregnant with terminological implications, was always 'should' and never 'sick aunt' or (alas, for the aunt) 'visit'?

But this was not to say that Speedfall never made up his mind, as though it were a bed that could not be made up because he was professionally lying in it all the time. He made it up frequently. And with frequently disastrous results.

First of all Speedfall decided that his colleagues must stop dithering about the Honorary Fellowship, as they had dithered about the stolen altarpiece, about the election of the Principal, about the sale of the Llanbadrig land, indeed as they had dithered about every issue that had come before them for as long as he could remember. Such dithering was an insult to the power of the human mind.

Then Speedfall decided to find a new Honorary Fellow for himself. It would have to be someone of immense academic authority, someone of acknowledged stature and achievement, who had for some peculiar reason been passed by. Preferably an old member of the College, of course, but otherwise the field was wide open. Speedfall was of the opinion that no one had looked farther than the end of his nose.

Actually, he didn't in the end need to look farther than his own nose, since the aforementioned sick aunt, who lived in Canterbury, sent him, quite without realising what excellent bait it was, the following cutting from the *Kentish Mercury*:

'MAD' SCIENTIST TRAPPED BY HIGH TIDE

14th May 'You probably think I'm mad' were the perceptive words with which Professor W. B. Manderson greeted the coastguards who today came to his rescue in Littlewich Bay, where he was trapped by the tide. Professor Manderson, who did not make his rescuers' task any lighter by refusing to abandon two large glass jars of sea water he was carrying, held the Chair of Zoology at the University of Stockport before he retired in 1949. He made his reputation with a study of the structure of marine organisms published in 1910 as a result of his work as a Junior Research Fellow of St Patrick's College, Oxford. In recent years he has turned his attention to human nutrition, and was a member of the United Nations Commission on World Food Resources in 1962. Professor Manderson lives with his sister at Mardow Manor, near Sandwich.

Speedfall was delighted. Billy Manderson, of course! How could they have forgotten old Manderson? Mad as a hatter now, unfortunately, but surely the most distinguished biologist in the country? It seemed incredible that someone of a slightly older generation than Haldane's should still be alive. Indeed, hadn't he for a while been Haldane's tutor? And wasn't there a rather malicious portrait of him in one of Aldous Huxley's novels? Speedfall asked Ted Wigan, the Marxist English Tutor, if he knew which one it was, but Wigan simply launched into an attack on poor Huxley:

'A classic example of what happened to the over-protected liberal humanist in the 'thirties,' he said through a mouthful of *sole doria*. 'No roots. A superstitious ostrich. Still essentially a late Victorian, of course.'

Speedfall had nodded absently, in no mood to argue with Wigan. He was reflecting that W. B. Manderson was himself essentially a late Victorian. His classic work on the structure of marine organisms (like D'Arcy Thompson's *On Growth and Form*, which was much indebted to it) had thrown phylogeny out of the window and substituted purely mathematical and ideal justifications for the shape of shells, for instance, or the arrangement of the spicules of hexactinellid sponges. It was beautifully written, and the drawings alone had kept the volume in print, but it was all as out of date as Norfolk jackets and penny-farthings, however compulsively new it had seemed at the time.

Manderson had caught up with biochemistry, of course, but he had never really specialised in that dogged way which confesses in humility and regret that the twentieth century scientist cannot know everything. Manderson *had* wanted to know everything. He had consistently related his subject to the larger world outside, and had just as consistently been exposed for it as a figure of fun. Well, not of fun exactly, since the newspapers loved him for the headlines he provided. Ask anyone old enough to remember when no one believed in the Loch Ness monster who first made *them* believe in it. Take a vote on who was the most amusing member of the original BBC Brains Trust. Mention, to anyone old enough to remember meat coupons, the simple phrase 'plankton sandwich'. Ask anyone over the age of thirty who it was who had burned his pension book on an Aldermaston march and had ousted Nasser from the front page of the *Daily Mirror*. The answer, of course, was W. B. Manderson.

The popular image was only the tip of an iceberg, Speedfall reflected. The man's career was deep and solid and vast enough. But would it withstand the glaring scrutiny of the St Patrick's Fellowship Committee, or would it simply melt away? He mentioned Manderson's name to Principal Crocusby.

'Good God,' said Crocusby. 'I thought he died years ago.'

When Speedfall said that Manderson had been a Research Fellow of the College, Crocusby looked him up.

'1908,' breathed the Principal, chuckling in disbelief. 'He was elected in February 1908!'

'The oldest, possibly the most distinguished ex-Fellow of the College, Maurice,' said Speedfall. 'Now, what about that Honorary Fellowship?'

'This is an Oxford College, not Madame Tussauds,' said Crocusby. But Speedfall could see that he was impressed.

Not like Curidge, the physiology tutor, who simply roared with laughter.

'Manderson?' he boomed, folding up his newspaper

decisively and smacking it down on the smoking-room table so that everyone turned to look. 'A simpleton, a delightful simpleton. Lived in a utopia of his own contrivance. Thought everyone was as simple as he was. Look at that letter to Stalin. Idiotic. Made him a laughing stock.'

On being told that Manderson was in fact alive and well, and living in Sandwich, Curidge raised a heavy pair of eyebrows.

'Is he, indeed?' he said. 'Well, well. Don't tell me that seaweed is good for you after all.'

Speedfall tried to find out from Curidge just what was wrong with seaweed, or with plankton for that matter, given the world's depleted food supplies. Hadn't it been an excellent notion of Manderson's to turn to such neglected sources of nutrition?

'All right if it *was* nutritious,' said Curidge. 'The trouble was getting hold of enough of the stuff to make it worth while. Even then it made people puke.'

Curidge contrived to dismiss most of Manderson's achievements as Speedfall mentioned them, but with such hostility that Speedfall became convinced that it was Manderson's politics rather than his research methods or scientific importance that was uppermost in his mind.

'If you can find just one invention of his that has done the world some good,' said Curidge smugly, 'I'll begin to believe that the old buffer is worth a fellowship. Not before.'

'Vitamin M?' suggested Speedfall.

Curidge merely grunted, and took up another newspaper.

Mardow Manor was a gaunt Victorian house built on a chalk bluff overlooking the River Stour. It had replaced a decayed Jacobean folly (there was still a pretty red-brick gazebo in the garden) and retained the air of eccentricity and aloofness that had inspired the original owner to seek such isolation. Speedfall, having dined and stayed over-night with his astonished and delighted aunt, was now to be found in earnest conversation with old Manderson and his sister in their garden.

'So you see,' he said, concluding an account of the College's inconclusive deliberations in which he himself figured largely as an admonitory and suffering conscience, 'I'm sure we'd be delighted to have you, if only . . .'

'If only anyone believed in me,' interrupted Manderson with a chuckle. He was tall and bony. Sitting in his deck-chair, his knees were almost level with his chin. He wore a floppy white hat of the kind that you see on children playing in sandpits.

'Nobody's ever believed in you except me,' said his sister shrilly.

'Be quiet, Dodo,' said Manderson. 'Why don't you go and bring some lunch?'

Dodo gave him a look which was a curious blend of a sweet smile and a suffering glare, and hobbled away across the lawn.

'You see, Speedfall,' said Manderson, rubbing his long nose. 'To be believed in, you've got to be in the swim. People have got to see that you're doing just the sort of thing that they would be doing if they were clever enough. They can't understand it at all if you're not, and they hate you for it.'

'Quite,' murmured Speedfall.

'And when they do catch up with you, they just pinch your work anyway.'

'Dear me,' said Speedfall.

'Well, I don't complain. I'm far too busy to worry about that.'

'I'm very glad to hear that you're still working.'

'What? Why on earth shouldn't I be working, eh?'

Manderson grinned, revealing an uninterrupted row of real though ancient teeth. Speedfall was amazed at how spry he seemed, and began to have some hopes that he might have a trick or two up his sleeve that would impress Curidge. They chatted on, and in a few minutes Dodo returned with a tray of sandwiches and a jug of cider.

'Very nice shrimp paste sandwiches,' said Speedfall with his mouth full.

Dodo snorted with laughter.

'Wriggly porridge!' she sang, to the tune of 'Hot Cross Buns.'

Speedfall smiled in puzzlement. He wasn't sure how to take this remark from the old lady. Though ten years younger than her brother, she was much more wizened, and seemed quite mad.

'Be quiet, Dodo,' said Manderson once again.

'Shan't,' she said. 'Why shouldn't he know that it's wriggly porridge?'

'What is wriggly porridge?' asked Speedfall uneasily.

'Worms, of course,' cried Dodo. 'You're eating worms!'

'Not at all,' put in Manderson unconvincingly. 'You're being very impolite to Mr Speedfall, Dodo.'

Dodo pouted.

Speedfall, by now thoroughly alarmed, took a gulp of cider. Manderson leaned over and patted him reassuringly on the arm.

'She always calls it that,' he said. 'Not to worry. She likes to tease.'

17

'What is it?' asked Speedfall, weakly.

'I thought I might show you after lunch, as a matter of fact,' said Manderson. 'Eat up. Oh, you've finished. Sure you don't want any more?'

Speedfall was quite sure.

True to his promise, Manderson led his guest away to his laboratory to show him the 'wriggly porridge', while Dodo cleared the plates in a sulk. The laboratory was actually situated in the old gazebo, and to Speedfall it was like entering the study of a Restoration virtuoso. It was a small octagonal building, and though full of tanks and wires, was as little like a modern laboratory as you could imagine.

'Do you find it easy to work here?' asked Speedfall.

'Couldn't work anywhere else. I need peace and quiet, and Dodo would never give it me if I worked in the house. Besides, she doesn't like coming here. She thinks it's going to fall over the cliff.'

Speedfall looked out of the mullioned window, and agreed that the view was splendid, if vertiginous, the river winding below through pasture and apple orchards.

'You see, it was perfectly feasible to lay on water and electricity from the house, and even more desirable to have a separate waste system here rather then use the sewer.'

Before Speedfall could ask why, Manderson had beckoned him to one of the largest of the tanks.

'You see, Speedfall,' he said, taking his elbow confidentially, 'I'm still working on this infernal problem of finding a new source of cheap food. I know it's got to come from the sea. Any child could tell you that. Look at a globe, for heaven's sake: it's all sea! Life came from the sea. It's a vast storehouse of natural food. The only trouble is harvesting it.'

'Like plankton?'

'Of course. Perfectly good idea, but uneconomic.'

Speedfall remembered what Curidge had said.

'Would people eat it?' he asked.

Manderson looked at him with withering scorn.

'Of course people would eat it,' he replied. 'People will eat anything when they've no unreasonable preconceptions about what it is. The problem is a purely practical one. Your lunch, for instance. You seemed to enjoy it?'

'Yes, indeed,' said Speedfall uncertainly.

'You see,' went on Manderson, 'I've realised that it's much better to breed the food than having to go out and collect it. Slow of me not to get on to that before. We had the problem originally when men turned from hunting to agriculture. It's the same thing.'

He pointed to the tank, which was half full of murky water.

'What you were eating was a particularly minute kind of sea-squirt which I have discovered in the caves along the coast here. It's the sort of creature you wouldn't normally notice: it's too small for the naked eye, and simply forms a sort of luminous slime on rocks. Rather elusive kind of food, you may think, but it happens to be extremely nutritious. What I had to do was to speed up its life cycle in order to get enough of it. You can do this now, of course, with the new chemical processes developed to encourage fertility. Difficult to apply it to such a tiny creature, but I've done it.'

Speedfall watched with a mixture of fascination and nausea as Manderson scooped some jelly-like substance from a flask and dropped it into the tank. Almost immediately it dispersed and the water became cloudier.

'You see,' said Manderson, 'I have the creatures in a

temporary sterile suspension in these storage flasks. Simply by reintroducing them into a saline environment I've made them go through their life cycle. A pretty tedious life it is, too. They begin as a sort of tadpole, with all the internal organs you'd expect in a small creature – gills, heart, intestine, eye, central nervous chord and so on, wriggling about like mad. Then they take a step back in the evolutionary scale, anchor themselves by the mouth to a rock, lose all these features and simply pump water in and out of themselves. Might as well be a vegetable.'

The walls of the tank were already coated with slime of a curious reddish-green colour.

'Tricky process,' said Manderson, fiddling with the terminals of a piece of electrical apparatus that stood nearby. 'They're living at a hundred times the usual rate, at least. As soon as they're established on the glass they start expelling eggs which mature in a matter of minutes. I began by scraping the squirts off the sides, but that only slowed the process down. As anchorage points become hard to find, they simply attach themselves to one another. Now I leave it till the tank is full.'

As the water thickened with the multiplying bodies of these minute creatures, so also it began to appear to move. At first it was only an imperceptible stirring, but soon it seethed and became more turbulent. It had also slowly risen, like boiling milk, and at a carefully judged moment Manderson plunged his electrode into the tank.

'You've got to kill the creatures before they get all over the place,' he said. 'Damn!'

Though the wriggly porridge was subsiding, some of it had splashed over the side of the tank and on to the table. Manderson peered at it closely.

'Still alive,' he said. 'You've got to be extremely careful when it gets out of the tank.'

He put his finger into the heaving pool on the table and licked it ruminatively.

'I think they really taste much better when electrocuted,' he said. 'Besides being easier to handle. Though if you poach the living ones the texture is a good deal smoother.'

This culinary point was lost on Speedfall, who was looking disgustedly at a blob of the wriggly stuff that had landed on his hand. He moved instinctively to the sink and turned on the tap.

'Leave it to dry,' began Manderson, but it was too late. Speedfall had rinsed his hand and the stuff had disappeared down the plughole.

'Not down the sink!' cried Manderson, moving to the door with an agility surprising for his age. 'Flaming hell! I should have warned you.'

Speedfall followed him in alarm round to the back of the gazebo and down a shaky wooden staircase that was attached uncertainly to the face of the cliff. Manderson raced ahead. He was half slithering down, with the rail beneath his armpit. Speedfall came down more heavily, splintering the rotten wood and missing his footing at every turn. 'What's the matter?' he panted.

At the bottom of the cliff was a large tank fed by the waste pipe that had descended parallel to the stair. Manderson knelt by it and turned a valve.

'Don't worry,' panted the old man. 'I'm always doing this myself and I'm sure I'm being overcautious, but just think what would happen if the stuff escaped into the river. Look.'

He lifted one of the wooden slats that covered the tank,

and Speedfall saw in the water a billowing and enlarging cloudy area of wriggly porridge.

'Caught it in time!' said Manderson. 'I turned off the valve to keep it in this tank. It's alive still, but it won't get much bigger than that. It needs salt water, you see.'

'And if it got out into the river?' asked Speedfall.

'Can't you imagine?' said Manderson. 'This is only a soakaway, but look how near the river is.'

They looked across a small field to where a pair of Friesians stood hock-deep in mud, swishing their tails in six-eight time against the maddening flies. Every now and again they lowered their sad heads to the surface of the river to drink.

'You saw how quickly the squirts developed in the tank? The established squirt goes on breeding, sending out eggs at regular intervals. No sexual problems at all. The population growth is astonishing, like bacteria.'

'And they'd survive in the river?' asked Speedfall.

'It's only a few miles to the coast and the salt environment they need, and then . . . well, it would depend on the time of the year and the currents. They're sensitive to temperature. But most of the ocean would turn into a sort of mayonnaise in about five days. The world's shipping would become marooned in mid-route. The weather would be quite unpredictable, though my guess is that we'd freeze in this country. When the squirts began to rot there'd be a tremendous hazard to health. That's one of the problems I'm working on now, because at the moment you can only eat the stuff as you breed it, within a few hours.'

Speedfall found himself with nothing to say. Could it really be that he had nearly clogged up the oceans with superfertile squirts by the simple gesture of washing his hand? It seemed unbelievable. He could imagine such a hazard closely controlled in a hygienic laboratory, full of chrome surfaces and white-coated assistants and elaborate procedures, but the idea that one nonagenarian in a gazebo could so threaten the world, in the nicest possible way, was something he didn't fully take in for some days.

Together they ascended the rickety wooden staircase.

'You can see now why I wanted a bit of control over the plumbing,' puffed Manderson as they climbed.

'Quite,' said Speedfall. 'What else can you do with the wriggly porridge?'

'What can't you do?' replied Manderson. 'Or rather, what can't Dodo do? It's very good in omelettes, and also delicious jellied, with the addition of aniseed or honey. She's also managed to dry it and pulverise it and make a kind of bread with it. She loves it like a baby.'

Speedfall, having recovered from the initial surprise of unwittingly eating the stuff and then having it wriggle about on his hand, was delighted. The rapid growth of the squirts seemed magical, while the implications (for a world three-quarters of whose population lived in danger of malnutrition or starvation) were staggering. Was not this the stuff of which Honorary Fellowships are made?

I suppose you have guessed what happened. Manderson had published almost nothing about his recent work, as he had been far too busy. He had told the press nothing, though there had been a flurry of interest after his episode in Littlewich Bay. He had, it is true, been in contact with Swansleigh, the food technician at the Bradford Polytechnic, but all in all it was quite clear to Speedfall that the discovery was woefully underpublicised. The due credit was not accruing, the starving millions were no closer to being fed and (worst of all) the way was not being paved for Speedfall's elderly protégé to attain his Fellowship.

Manderson himself, of course, didn't have much time for Fellowships and showed Speedfall far too little gratitude for his efforts, the latter thought. There was one very good reason, however, why he might wish to be given one, and that was to escape from the increasingly unreliable and interfering ministrations of Dodo. On being told that not only would he be given his own room in college, but that St Patrick's actually possessed a small laboratory in which he could perfect the breeding and control of the squirts, his eyes had lit up – and he had raised no further objection to being groomed and coached for the election.

What Speedfall had omitted to mention was that Curidge had for many years used the college laboratory for the instruction of his own pupils in those subjects for which he felt the faculty provisions were inadequate. He had also set up there his own dissecting room, and a private den where he kept his old collection of stag-beetles (including *Lucanus Curidgeanus*, discovered while still an undergraduate and dabbling in entomology), a locked cupboard full of gin, and shelf upon shelf of periodicals. His college room was sparely but elegantly furnished; it could not suffer the intrusion of such utilitarian lumber.

Speedfall had little sympathy for Curidge. Why should any Fellow have in effect two rooms? There was no provision for it in either Statute or By-Law. It was surely appropriate that a venerable new Honorary Fellow (though not yet actually elected) should be able to lay claim to the laboratory and its offices in order to develop the distinguished work upon which that expected election rested?

Thus he argued to Principal Crocusby, and thus was Principal Crocusby, who so frequently took the line of least resistance, inclined to agree.

He did suggest, however, that it would assist the Fellowship Committee to come to a conclusion if Manderson could be persuaded to come up to Oxford to give a demonstration. It would be nothing like an interview, naturally, for that would be most improper. It shouldn't appear to have anything at all to do with the Fellowship. But it would pave the way for the election, especially considering the opposition being put up by Curidge.

Luckily (or perhaps unluckily) Curidge was not himself on the Fellowship Committee, and thus for a time his antagonism to Manderson expressed itself only in irritable outbursts in Common Room.

'I see the old Bolshevik is actually bringing his worm farm to St Patrick's,' he would say. Or: 'We're to become a sub-department of the Ministry of Agriculture and Fisheries, I hear.'

When the time came for the demonstration, the sarcasm had given way to an icy and more dangerous calm. Speedfall had offered to drive down again to Mardow Manor to fetch Manderson and his flasks and any other equipment that could not easily be duplicated to his instructions in the St Patrick's laboratory. They arrived on a Tuesday evening in pouring rain in the college car park with the boot and the back seat crammed full. Manderson was all for getting the stuff installed in the laboratory right away, and tottered off across the tarmac towards a couple of undergraduates who were tinkering with a bicycle in one of the sheds that stood nearby. Of course they were willing to help, but did he mind awfully if they got the Raleigh assembled first, or else the parts would get kicked around and lost? Speedfall came up, saw the rain dripping off the end of Manderson's nose and promptly arranged for the undergraduates to reappear after Hall to carry the equipment. The first thing was clearly to get the old man safely to his guest room in the rear quad and perhaps to offer him a hot bath. His things would be safe enough in the car until after dinner.

But they weren't. After dinner three of the flasks were missing, Manderson became distraught, the demonstration was abandoned and the election to the Honorary Fellowship not made. I don't think much more was heard of Manderson's squirts, because he died the following year. Dodo went into a home at Ashford, and Mardow Manor became an institute for the deaf.

Nothing was done about the stolen flasks. It wasn't that it was at all doubtful who had taken them. Speedfall was perfectly certain that Curidge had taken them, though the Principal was inclined to doubt it and to let sleeping dogs lie and so forth. Nothing official was done, except that the matter was ineffectually investigated by the Dean, for form's sake. Speedfall wanted to call in the police, but Manderson, whose distraction and alarm had almost immediately been followed by depression and fatigue, absolutely forbade it. The squirts would not live for more than a week in suspended animation in the flasks, and would not therefore be a permanent danger. He could get hold of more, and the process of treating them only took a few weeks. He was tired and wanted to go home.

There the matter seemed to have abruptly ended except that Speedfall did eventually confront Curidge about the theft. Since I'm absolutely terrified of Curidge myself at the best of times and would never even sit next to him at lunch if I could help it, this enormously impressed me. It would take a philosopher to do it, of course.

'It strikes me that the person to gain most from the disappearance of Manderson's flasks is likely to have taken them,' he said.

Curidge merely raised his eyebrows, his customary gesture of disbelief, amusement or scorn.

'It also seems clear to me,' went on Speedfall, 'that whoever would have been most put to a disadvantage by Manderson's probable election would gain most from the disappearance of his flasks.'

'Yes?' scowled Curidge.

'Further consideration of the problem would prompt one to suggest that the greatest disadvantage arising from Manderson's possible election lay in his requirement of the college laboratory for his work.'

'What are you implying?' asked Curidge.

'Nothing at all,' said Speedfall. 'I am in fact expressly maintaining that the thief and the present user of the laboratory stand in the relation of identity.'

'Speak English, man,' snapped Curidge. 'You're saying I took those damned bottles, are you?'

Speedfall blinked.

'Yes,' he said.

Curidge roared with laughter.

'Well, what if I did?' he said. 'The whole thing was a farrago of nonsense anyway. I did the college a service.'

Speedfall ignored this bluster.

'What did you do with them?' he asked in a low voice.

'Oh, they're safe enough. But I got rid of that beastly brew.'

'How?'

'Poured it down the lavatory.'

Speedfall went white and opened his mouth, but nothing came out. He was trying to work out how long it took for the Isis to flow to the sea, and what actually happened to sewage when it was treated (hadn't Manderson avoided using the sewer as an outlet?) and whether he should ring up Manderson, or the Home Office or whatever.

In the end he rather uncharacteristically did nothing. He watched the papers closely for a sign of the global seize-up that Manderson had predicted, but there was nothing except an article on the problems of de-silting the Thames estuary, which must have been written long before Curidge had launched the squirts on their possibly triumphal and apocalyptic journey. In the bad dreams he began to have at that time, Dodo Manderson would come very close to him, grinning, with an open toothless mouth ready to fasten on to him. Or he would find himself sitting at a large mahogany table up to his knees in water at a formal high Victorian dinner, while powdered footmen brought round tureens of unspeakable soup.

You will say that Speedfall was pulling my leg, but it all fitted in with what I knew myself about Manderson's visit to St Patrick's, and besides, Speedfall has no sense of humour whatsoever. It would be beyond him to tease me so elaborately.

Incidentally, the death of the Bishop of Reading (a man remembered not for his theology but for his ability to complete *The Times* crossword puzzle in six and a half minutes) suddenly solved the problem of the Honorary Fellowship. There were now *two* statutory vacancies, so that the Prime Minister and the Leader of the Opposition were both after all elected. It was felt that an abundance of ancient claret would be likely to obviate their political animosity, and at any rate, it was argued, to elect both showed the college's own fine political wisdom. It demonstrates that all insoluble problems can usually somehow be solved. And most disasters turn out to be not so dreadful after all.

I thought that would be the end of it, but I've just this minute seen an article in the latest *Scientific American* about an unaccountable and alarming rise in sea-level – almost three-quarters of an inch in just less than a year. God knows how they measure it. The article seems to suggest that a change in temperature and consequent melting of ice *could* account for the rise, but goes on to say that the polar caps are in fact extending themselves rather than shrinking. They don't seem to have a reasonable explanation of it at all.

I hope it's not wriggly porridge.

The Mongolian Gambit Declined, Robinson Defence

To be fair, the whole business was really the fault of Speedfall's uncle. So Speedfall maintained, and I could hardly deny it. Though with such a nephew to exacerbate and perpetuate any slight initial misunderstanding there may have been, who needed the uncle or the slight initial misunderstanding in the first place? The mayhem that generally attended my colleague was so frequently self-generating that particular excuses seemed, in the end, though perfectly justifiable, somehow beside the point. And in any case, Speedfall was blessed with a trickier set of uncles and aunts than you usually encounter in a family tree, due in the main (he claimed) to the rude health and animal inclinations of his paternal grandfather coupled with the feckless compliance and educational incompetence of his paternal grandmother.

The uncle in question, who had at an early age elbowed his way to the top of this heap of indulged siblings, was Sir Jeremy Speedfall. Sir Jeremy had continued to elbow. He had elbowed at Cambridge, and in his Department when he stayed on to do research; he had elbowed during the War; he had elbowed vigorously in his Ministry. He was so good at elbowing that he could elbow by lifting his eyebrows. He could, without the least effort, even lift his eyebrows over the telephone, so that a call from Sir Jeremy was from long habit a matter of wielded elbows.

Therefore, when one morning early last Trinity Term Speedfall was interrupted in the middle of a tutorial by a distantly affable and semi-audible Sir Jeremy, he didn't (as he would have done for anyone else) ask him to ring back, but cradled the telephone patiently while his uncle breezed on with some elaborate request.

'What's that, Uncle Jeremy?' said Speedfall, while trying to indicate with his free hand that his pupil should not simply stare into space during this temporary respite but continue with the exercises they had been looking at. 'What did you say? Your team? You want me to look after them?'

The voice bayed indistinctly at the other end of the line.

'When are they coming, Uncle Jeremy? I see. What? God, no, I don't see how I can put them up here. What?'

The voice, without perceptibly altering in pitch, began to sound distinctly elbowish. The pupil was drawing circles with his pencil.

'Well, I don't know. Yes, of course. All right, yes. Yes, I see. Very important. Quite.'

Speedfall glared down the telephone, and then glared at his pupil, who put the pencil to one side and began to stare at Speedfall's kettle.

'Uncle Jeremy, of course,' said Speedfall unctuously, 'that's just the sort of thing I can do. Yes! Of course I want to help. Quite. Mongolian, you say? Tuesday. I'll ring you later. Not to bother? The ten-fifteen? I see. Right. Well, goodbye, Uncle Jeremy. Thank you.'

It is said (the pupil of course being the authority) that Speedfall's glare gradually mellowed during this conversation into an abject and benign grin, like that of a terrier ready to fetch his master's slippers.

I was actually present when the Mongolian party first arrived at St Patrick's. Speedfall had evidently failed to meet their train, for they turned up at the Lodge alone and lost. I was there collecting my mail from my pigeon-hole when they trooped in, like Japanese tourists (minus the cameras and waterproof hats). Their leader, who was the spitting image of Billie-Jean King, except for the fact that he had the eyebrows of Lord Goodman, smiled peacefully at the porter.

'I'm afraid the College is closed until two o'clock, sir,' said Marshal, lifting a very sharp pencil three inches from the counter between them and replacing it at an angle of forty-five degrees from its former position as though he were adjusting a delicate chronometer.

All the Mongolians smiled broadly at this and nodded several times. Their leader said (at least, the following sounds occurred somewhere in the space between him and Marshal, without breaking the steady diplomatic gleam of his teeth):

'Roxfor see Peefor, please.'

Marshal prided himself on his ability to deal in a firm and friendly way with all difficult visitors to the Lodge (drunks, mothers, undergraduates from other colleges requiring the squash-court keys, maniacs, and so forth) and said promptly:

'Ah, yes, indeed it is, sir. You'll just have to come back at two o'clock.'

'Dr Peefor,' ventriloquised Billie-Jean King. 'Roxfor tray.'

'Only at weekends, I'm sorry to say, sir,' said Marshal, brightly. He was getting out of his depth, so I thought I had better step in. He seemed much relieved when I did.

'Is Dr Speedfall expecting you?' I asked.

The Mongolians, who were already nodding, nodded more quickly, like a shelf-ful of curios set in motion by a bored shopkeeper.

'I can show you where his room is, if you like,' I offered.

But there was no need, as it happened, for me to embark on the difficult business of shepherding this lot into the tortuous depths of the College, for at that moment Speedfall himself burst into the Lodge. It seems that he thought they were to catch the 10.15 from London, whereas they must have caught the nine-something arriving at 10.15. It was a good job he had checked his timetable a few minutes ago or else he might have missed them entirely, he said, shaking them all by the hand.

'Peefor?' said Billie-Jean King's clenched teeth. 'Cheerio!'

He bowed, and began to effect introductions, the limited syllables of his party's names sounding as cunningly varied and combined as a peal of bells. While they were picking up their small cardboard suitcases and working out whose was whose, Speedfall turned to me in despair:

'They can't even speak English!' he hissed. 'What can I do with them?'

I shrugged and smiled.

'You must help me out,' he said. 'I've got the kitchen to lay on a spot of lunch in the Beaumont Room. Do join us.'

I began to make excuses.

'There's claret,' added Speedfall.

He looked so sorry for himself that I relented. I was in any case curious to know what he intended to do with the

Mongolians, and if I got bored I could always leave. I said I would turn up at one o'clock, after the last tutorial of the morning.

'Excellent,' said Speedfall.

When I arrived, a little late, at his buffet lunch, I found the Mongolians with their noses in glasses of claret, still smiling, as though they had been handed not wine but the paraphernalia of some jolly party game. Other entertainment was provided in the shape of Prendergast, the Tutor in Anatomy, who scowled in a corner; and Curidge, tall and elegant, talking metabolism over the sleek head of Billie-Jean King. The latter took little notice of Curidge's monologue, of which he evidently understood not a word, but smiled and touched the meniscus of his claret with his forefinger as if to test its temperature.

'Please!' he said to Curidge's moving chin.

The chin continued to move, and an agreeable stream of information about current personalities, learned articles, withheld grants, impending lectures and unresolved controversies on the subject of metabolism, flowed from his claret-moistened lips.

'Cheerio!' said Billie-Jean King, hopefully.

'Er, indeed,' said Curidge, lifting his glass. He swivelled on his heel, looking amongst the assembled company for someone who might be a little more receptive. His search was disappointed.

Speedfall was engaged with another of the party, who, except for an outsize drooping moustache of the Charles Bronson variety, did not look more than ten years old. I took a glass myself and offered a few remarks to three Mongolians who were standing somewhat apart together, stealing pieces of ham from the side table. They giggled, but said nothing in reply. They were standing so near together that they looked as though they were about to break into song: from the archaic cut of their jackets, all of identical cheap shiny pale blue, with enormous padded shoulders, it would have been some sort of Bepob of the late Forties, a close-harmony group like the Inkspots. I almost wished they would, for I had ground to a conversational halt myself.

But pretty soon we were saved by the entry of Ferguson with a tray of hot rolls and baked potatoes and one or two other dishes that seemed to indicate that the table was now complete. Speedfall exclaimed in tones of undisguised relief: 'Aha! Now please help yourselves, gentlemen!' The Tutor in Anatomy already had his plate half-filled. There was a general move towards the food.

Speedfall took the opportunity to take me into a corner.

'It's worse than I thought,' he hissed. 'Much, much worse.'

'Why?' I asked. 'They seem a rather choice crew to me. Why not make the most of them? Good for a few laughs.'

'You don't understand,' replied Speedfall. 'I must have got it all wrong. They're not what I thought they were. Uncle Jeremy said would I look after his team on a visit to Oxford. Naturally I thought they'd be visiting Professor Haifisch's department. He's heard nothing about it. And it's quite clear to me – it would be perfectly clear to anyone – that they're not medics at all!'

'I see,' I said. 'You thought they'd be boffins from the Ministry.'

'Well, naturally . . .'

'But why on earth should your Uncle Jeremy have a team of Mongolians working for him?'

'You don't know Uncle Jeremy,' said Speedfall ruefully.

'I don't, as a matter of fact,' I said, with as much sympathy as I could muster. 'Does any of this matter?'

Speedfall's voice dropped an octave or so, as though he had entered a mosque, and he gripped my elbow.

'Matter? Of course it matters,' he whispered, in sepulchral tones. 'I depend on Uncle Jeremy. In more ways than you can imagine.'

'He'll cut you off without a penny?'

'There's no need to make a comedy out of it,' snapped Speedfall.

'I wasn't,' I said.

'What can I do?'

'Ring your uncle now, and find out just who they are and what they expect here.'

'I can't do that. That's the worst thing I could do.'

'Well, then, get hold of one of them and ask. I can't see that they could take offence.'

'I don't think I'd get very far, do you?'

I was forced to agree. Perhaps Speedfall would never find out who they were or what they expected. I didn't exactly care myself, but (as with all of Speedfall's adventures) the affair had a certain mild interest of a bizarre kind.

However, he was thrown a lifeline by the one with the Charles Bronson moustache, who took him to one side and murmured in a voice that sounded as if it came from under water:

'Please?'

'Ah, yes,' said Speedfall briskly, in pleased anticipation of being asked something for a change.

'Roxfor,' said Bronson. 'Good sess?'

Speedfall stared at him for a moment, in a semantic no-man's-land.

'Sess?' he repeated. Then light dawned, and he glanced at me conspiratorially. 'Absolutely.'

Charles Bronson grinned happily.

'Chess,' went on Speedfall in an ecstasy of understanding, 'is just what we're terribly good at here at Oxford. You do mean chess, don't you? Rook, queen, pawn, you know?'

He accompanied his last remark with little lunges of his fingers as though moving chess pieces. Bronson, across whose face had appeared a momentary flicker of doubt, was now enthusiastic.

'Please!' he nodded. 'Rook queer porn? Roxfor.'

He said something to the Inkspots, who joined him in a chorus of coos and nods.

'Of course,' said Speedfall in an undertone to me. 'I should have realised, when Uncle Jeremy said "team". They're a visiting chess team! He's a strong player himself, you know. Once did something quite brilliant at Hastings in the Fifties. Drew with Smyslov, I think.'

'Are you quite sure?' I asked. The Inkspots were making movements with their fingers like the movements Speedfall had made, but not quite like them, and the expression of ecstatic anticipation on their faces seemed to me to have not much to do with that noblest of intellectual pursuits.

'I see what you mean,' replied Speedfall, not seeing at all. He turned to Charles Bronson. 'You do play Western chess, of course? You play the game as we do? Queen, bishops, rooks and so forth? Two knights and all that?'

Bronson beamed and giggled.

'Queer Roxfor bishops,' he agreed. 'Game! Two nights game! Cheerio!'

In his conviction that he now had the complete answer to the Mongolian Problem, Speedfall was deaf to anything they actually said. He filled everyone's glass himself, his brain buzzing with plans for a College chess match to please and entertain these visiting prodigies.

'Roscar Wilde,' intoned Bronson, twirling the stem of his claret with mock elegance. Speedfall moved among the group with the liberal decanter, hearing nothing.

'Reveryn Waugh. Max Barebum.'

There was nothing I could do to stop him.

It appears that Speedfall set about organising the chess match within the hour, leaving his visitors in the Smoking Room to doze off the effect of their lunch. He wasn't entirely sure who to ask at first, but met Prettihow on the croquet lawn, was reminded by this that Prettihow spent all his afternoons on the croquet lawn playing his pupils with a tiny mallet and an immense frown, and concluded that anyone who did that probably played other games as well.

Prettihow said he hadn't played for years, but was a tolerable hand at bridge. Why didn't Speedfall ask one of the Maths tutors? Speedfall sighed. The Maths tutors were elusive creatures. He left Prettihow savagely belting his opponent's ball into the wallflowers and went to knock on Campling's door.

Campling happened to be in, staring at an empty blackboard in the corner of his room. He is one of the shyest Fellows of the College, and it took him some time to say anything at all in reply to Speedfall's request. But he agreed to play in a match after dinner. Just as Speedfall was leaving he suggested (with a reluctance and deference that left the remark all but inaudible) that the man who should really be asked was Professor Nought. Nought was certainly high priority. He'd once played for his country. Ask him.

Nought was harder to track down, since Professors do not teach undergraduates and are rarely to be found in their college rooms. Speedfall dashed up Parks Road, and took the short cut through Museum Road to the Mathematics Institute. Was Nought in his room there? He was; and he was also staring at a blackboard in the corner of his room. But there were some scrawled figures on his blackboard, looking for all the world like the results of a Lebanese football match. There was something uncanny about the similar posture and activity, as though Campling and he were experimenting in extra-sensory perception, a sort of blackboard bush-telegraph.

Nought knew Speedfall quite well, since they shared an interest in logic. He unfolded his arms, therefore, pulled his glasses down from the dome of his head on to his nose, and became affable. Chess? Wonderful. Always glad to play a game of chess. Had Speedfall asked Prettihow? And the Bursar? And were they allowed to have undergraduates?

Speedfall was certain that they were allowed to have undergraduates. They must make up the best possible College team.

Then Speedfall must have T. G. R. Robinson, third-year Maths and Economics.

Then Speedfall would indeed have T. G. R. Robinson, if Robinson was good.

Robinson was good, was extremely good, in fact. He had beaten John Nunn at least once, and last year had a rating of 221. It was imperative to have Robinson (and there were a couple of other undergraduates worth getting, too) but there was one problem. Robinson had been rusticated for the term.

Professor Nought seemed pleased to impart this information, since he smiled sardonically, and folded his arms again.

'Rusticated?' exclaimed Speedfall in dismay.

'You ought to know,' replied Professor Nought. 'You're on the Tutors' Committee, aren't you? I'm not.'

'What was he rusticated for?'

'Goodness knows. You'll have to hold the match on neutral territory.'

'Can't be done.'

'Well, fix it with the Dean, then. I'll turn up after dinner, shall I?'

Speedfall established the time and place, revisited Prettihow (who was reaching into the wallflowers for his own ball), caught the Bursar climbing into his Peugot, and persuaded the Dean to de-rusticate Robinson for the day.

'Perfectly all right with me,' said the Dean, 'but do try to get the villain out by midnight, will you, and see that he stays out?'

Nothing easier, thought Speedfall, but how was he going to find Robinson? The afternoon had slipped by, and the pupil he had bribed to show the Mongolians the College's architectural splendours reported that he could stand it no longer, darkly hinting that he was being assailed by something worse than boredom.('Take them on the river, anything,' pleaded Speedfall, 'and you needn't write next week's essay.') Like many passing and unforeseen ordeals, this one had completely taken over Speedfall's existence. If he had paused to calculate the precise degree of coolness and displeasure on his uncle's part likely if he did nothing for the Mongolians but ply them with claret and have them taken on the river, he would have shrugged and abandoned his quest for half-a-dozen top-notch chess-players at such short notice, as being by no means cost-effective. As it was, he had been visited with a revelation which, in its brilliant solution of his social difficulty, seemed to require fulfilment and realisation for its own sake.

Thus he found himself in the early evening outside a brick terrace in south-west Oxford ringing on a bell as small (and as apparently inaudible) as the end of a retractable ball-point pen. After several silent and increasingly hopeless rings, he heard an upper window open and a rather nasal horsy Kingston-upon-Thames sort of voice call out: 'Is that you, Fergus?'

Speedfall stepped back on to the pavement and looked up, but the owner of the voice had disappeared. After a few moments the door opened, and a scowling girl with black lipstick and a green crew-cut stood before him. She was wearing what appeared to be a soft leather suitcase, complete with straps, locks and handles, as though she had just packed herself up to be taken away and hadn't quite managed to get her head in.

'Oh, bugger,' she said in her incongruously well-tailored voice, 'I thought you were Fergus.'

Speedfall apologised for not being Fergus, and asked for Robinson. Robinson was not there. Robinson was possibly with Fergus, and Fergus (since Speedfall was not Fergus) was probably at the K.A. If Robinson was with Fergus, he would (probably) find it difficult to get him away. But she would be glad if Speedfall would try, because Fergus would stay there as long as Robinson did and Robinson would stay there as long as Fergus did, and Fergus was (possibly) going to take her out to dinner and unless alternative entertainment was found for Robinson it looked as though he (probably) wouldn't.

Speedfall, reckoning her in the circumstances a likely ally, told her about the chess match and invited her to join her search for Fergus with his for Robinson. She agreed, and together they made for the King's Arms.

There were the pair of them on the pavement in the late sunlight (as was the habit of many of the K.A. regulars) quaffing pints of Wadworth's 6X. Fergus was bald and earringed, Robinson merely shabby. They seemed neither pleased nor unpleased to have been discovered, though they found it difficult to conceal their amusement at the presence of Speedfall.

Robinson, though unshaven and hollow-eyed (looking indeed rather as if he were well into the sixth week of a hunger-strike) and though so drunk that he had to close his eyes for about half a minute at the end of every sentence, drove as hard and lucid a bargain as the secretary of a Miners' Union. The most that Speedfall could do was to convince him that a permanent de-rustification was beyond his power to effect, and Robinson was not sure after a few minutes lowering of the eyelids that he would want that anyway, because it would mean seeing his tutor again and he rather liked life without Campling. It therefore became a question of money: more than one fiver would have to change hands if he were to deign to turn out for the College against the Mongolians. Speedfall sighed, and agreed.

'But will you be fit to play?' he added.

'You mean this?' asked Robinson, lifting his nearly empty glass. 'Oh, I shall need lots of this. I play much better when I'm tanked up. And I'd like Fergus to come.'

It was agreed that Fergus should come, and (after some mild disagreement on her part) that the Suitcase should accompany him.

'I shall feel a good deal safer,' said Robinson wearily, draining his glass and handing it to Speedfall to be refilled.

When the Mongolians saw the row of chessboards laid out after dinner in the Beaumont Room they seemed disappointed and puzzled. They had been brought in from the river in euphoric mood by Speedfall's pupil, who was disinclined to give any explanation of his torn shirt or the grass in his hair. They had drunk plentifully at dinner, and although Billie-Jean King had been unable to say anything very much to the Dean, he had shown a great interest in the Dean's left elbow, while the Inkspots had ogled Principal Crocusby, and Charles Bronson asked the Under Butler more than once if he was related to, or perhaps was, Roscar Wilde.

Those Fellows who had agreed to play were either too nervous of their own performance or too ready to believe in the brilliance of Speedfall's visitors to feel that anything was amiss. They even accepted the colourful arrival of Fergus and the Suitcase as somehow appropriate to the occasion, as though such a formal and quasi-medieval tourney needed a touch of motley. And the Mongolians brightened up considerably when Robinson and his friends came in, feeling perhaps that the business with the boards was, after all, to be simply a necessary prologue to the main excitement of the evening, like the bidding at a slave auction.

I went along myself, not so much out of loyalty to Speedfall as out of an intense curiosity to see how the misunderstanding would resolve itself. For what the Mongolians were really after was not something that Speedfall could provide; and it didn't seem likely that they could rise convincingly to the business at hand, which their eager host had spent so much energy in contriving.

Could the Mongolian Chess Team actually play chess? The answer to this question was not as easy to arrive at as you might think. The order of the boards fell out as follows: Bronson was to play Robinson, Billie-Jean King was to play Professor Nought and the Inkspots were put into the care of Campling, Prettihow and the Bursar. I didn't believe that the Bursar was any good at all; Prettihow's arms were well programmed to make strokes with a mallet but not to move small pieces of black and white wood; and Campling, who hardly ever spoke in any case, was not likely to complain about the quality of the opposition. Professor Nought was always so pleased with himself, so certain of his charm and his abilities, that he would never have admitted to what would inevitably look like a calculated insult to himself. That left Robinson, who would have no illusions about the Emperor's Clothes, and would in any case be eager to expose Speedfall (and through him, his tutor Campling), and to make a laughingstock of the College.

It was at the top board that the onlookers gathered, as being the likely source of the greatest brilliance. Fergus occasionally wandered down to the third board (no doubt under instructions from Robinson) to breathe irritatingly down Campling's neck; and the occasional burst of hysterical laughter drew glances at Prettihow who sat at the fourth board, flushed and weak with his own incompetence; but attention was in the main focussed on Robinson, for word of his ability had circulated, and the Principal himself entered the room as the opponents made their first moves, rubbing his hands and expressing his hope to the company that Speedfall's visitors would be soundly trounced.

If Bronson had ever seen a chess board before, he successfully disguised the fact from me, at any rate. He looked down on the twin phalanxes of pieces with the frustration and eagerness of appetite of a man presented with his third dozen of oysters and no means of opening them. He stared at Fergus and the Suitcase, and back at the board, as though they contained some clue as to what was required. The Mongolians were playing white on the top board, black on the second, and so on. Professor Nought had already moved P–K4 on the second board. Everyone waited. Bronson waited. He seemed to be waiting for Robinson to move, until Robinson opened his haggard eyes and looked at him expectantly.

The Suitcase giggled. Bronson, interpreting this as some sort of erotic signal, beamed broadly, and in a sudden access of enthusiasm and goodwill did what he had seen Professor Nought do with his white King's pawn – nudged it forward two squares.

The game had begun.

Nothing happened for a while, because Robinson's eyelids had dropped again, but as soon as they rose he observed the board with the attention it deserved. I could see him hesitate with Gallic nicety over the French Defence, and I fancied (as the bruised eyes focussed upon the King's Knight) that he pondered for a moment the cunning seduction of Alekhine's Defence. His glance strayed to his right, and a sort of Mafia scowl attended his entertainment of the Sicilian: but he did not move his Queen's Bishop's Pawn. A flicker crossed his face: was he considering the Pirc? No. The onlookers wondered what astounding move Robinson had up his sleeve as he kept them all in suspense. His fingers hovered over the board, and he moved.

Pawn to King Four, like his opponent.

A mild sigh of mingled relief, disappointment, recognition and approval came from those standing behind him, and his heavy eyelids drooped once more.

Bronson seemed pleased at this corroboration of the suitability of pushing one of the little pieces forward two squares, and promptly did the same with the next one on the right. Pawn to King's Bishop Four: the King's Gambit. I privately guessed, however, that it was in this case so unintended that it might just as well have been rechristened the Mongolian Gambit.

Robinson had a clearer idea of how to cope with this. He would not accept the pawn, but moved his own Pawn to Queen Four: the Falkbeer Countergambit.

'Things are going swimmingly, I must say,' Speedfall whispered to me, a decanter in his hand. 'Claret?'

It was a decidedly better claret than the one we had had at lunch, and, like most of the company, I was glad of a glass. Not so Robinson, who looked up at Speedfall with the mournful pallor of a Zurbaran hermit and asked for some Wadsworth's instead. Being the hoped-for hero of the hour and so forth, Speedfall set about obliging him.

Bronson, meanwhile, perceiving that his opponent had moved two pawns forward like himself and that therefore there could be very little wrong with this procedure, pushed forward a third. Pawn to King's Knight Four: his beam deepened, as though having discovered the simple secret of the game, he was ready to go on playing it all night.

Consternation! What could he mean by it? Robinson

frowned. He twitched slightly, and ran his fingers through his uncombed and uncut hair. Why was his opponent laying open his King's side like this? It was unheard of. He laid his fingertips on the edge of the table and bent over it, looking as though he were playing the Moonlight Sonata, rather than a game of Mongolian chess. What was he to do? He still did not want the originally offered pawn, and didn't like the idea of doubled pawns on his King's file (he had, of course, been expecting Bronson to take the Queen's pawn). He decided, quite properly in my view, to develop his minor pieces on the King's side. Mayhem amongst White's pawns by Queen to Rook Five (check) was clearly a wonderful temptation, and I suppose most players would have cheerfully undertaken it. But Robinson knew very well the danger of exposing the Queen too early, and was not going to be lured into any wily oriental trap. He therefore moved his King's Knight to Bishop Three, hoping, I imagined, to secure King Five in the first instance rather than Knight Five, if his rash opponent were to move Pawn to Bishop Five.

Since Robinson had moved his Knight, so did Bronson. In fact he made the identical move, Knight to King's Bishop Three. I still didn't know whether or not he was learning the moves as he went along.

Robinson was even more puzzled by this, for now the Knight's pawn was en prise. Without much hesitation, he took it with his bishop.

I could see Bronson's little eyes light up at this: yet another kind of move! He lifted his King's Bishop and slid it diagonally as far as it would go to the right. It didn't go very far, ending up at Rook Three.

Robinson was thoroughly rattled at this. He couldn't

believe his eyes at first; then he suspected a trap. But no: it really did seem that the bishop was on offer, with no immediate retribution. Some of the onlookers were puzzled, too, but I think that most of them had come prepared to witness some deep play, and did not dare be critical of any move, however surprising. It was a different matter for Robinson, though. He looked for his beer, but none had arrived yet, so he reached for the nearest wine-glass and drained it. Then he took the bishop.

Did Bronson realise that it wasn't, on the whole, a good idea to lose his pieces? I don't know. In fact I'm quite uncertain as to what exactly was going on in his head. At the time I was convinced that the whole business was for him simply an elaborate and comic preliminary to something more exciting, rather like a Geisha tea-ceremony or something of that sort. Later, I wasn't so sure.

For his next move (having run out of novelties, it seems) he reverted to the pawn-pushing, and put his Queen's Pawn at Queen Four.

Robinson began to look around him – for help, I thought, or some corroboration that this was not quite the calibre of match he had expected. But he was on his own. He took another glass of wine, therefore, shuddering slightly. It was probably at this point that his control of the game began to slip. His next move, Knight to Knight Five, didn't seem quite right to me. I didn't see why he didn't take the pawn. But the general principle of opening the Queen's diagonal to Rook Five seemed useful enough, given the harrowing vulnerability of White's King's side.

Bronson, apparently pleased by symmetry, also moved Knight to Knight Five. Was it such a parrot-like move? The Queen's diagonal was closed and Robinson now had to do something with the bishop which was under attack. Mind you, Bronson looked quite unconcerned, and I was sure that if Robinson were to leave the bishop where it was it would be quite safe. But Bishop to Knight Seven, attacking Bronson's rook, was possible – so he made the move.

Speedfall appeared with Robinson's beer, half of which disappeared almost at one gulp, and was just in time to witness the first move of Bronson's which could not have been pure mimicry: Rook to Knight One. It cast much doubt on my private theory that he was simply extemporising, although it is true that he had already seen the bishop make a capture similar to that threatened, and so to move the rook out of the way was simple common sense.

The beer did Robinson no good at all. He looked as though he had been woken in the middle of the night with news of the Third World War. What had been the point of moving the bishop? If captured by the Knight, he could check with his Queen at Rook Five and regain the piece. He moved the bishop back. And Bronson them moved his rook back! Robinson's next move was devious to the point of puerility: Pawn to King's Bishop Four. It made a nice pattern of pawns in the centre, and no doubt encouraged his opponent to believe in the continued efficacy of the tank-like move of a pawn to the fourth rank, but what did it achieve? I could see that it protected his knight, and I could see that if he now lost his bishop, Queen to Rook Five created trouble for White. But at the same time I felt that he had been lulled into a secure belief that his opponent was mad and was unlikely to do anything constructive or useful.

I didn't care what was happening elsewhere, though a

manic laugh from Prettihow did for a moment make me wonder what forms of anarchy were occurring on the other boards. I don't think that Fergus was much interested in any of it, for he had begun to massage the Suitcase's neck with one hand, rather as if he were tightening a screw that held her together, and she was giving the occasional little shrug and murmur as if she were not quite sure that she needed to be prevented from falling apart.

Bronson noticed all this, and became quite excited.

'Cheerio!' he said, with a leer, making his next move with a nonchalant gallantry.

It was Pawn to Queen's Bishop Four. Robinson closed his eyes again for a full fifteen seconds, opened them, looked at the board, and finished his beer. He was thoroughly demoralised by now, and unprepared to take the time necessary to work out how to resolve the temporarily stone-walled pawns. He simply supported his Queen's pawn (Pawn to Queen's Bishop Three) and gave his empty glass to Speedfall with a dog-like and silent appeal for it to be refilled.

'Is that a good idea?' I whispered to Speedfall.

'Why not?' was the reply. 'He told me that he played at his best when drinking beer.'

'And when mixing it with claret, too?' I replied.

'Oh dear,' said Speedfall. 'I didn't realise that. He's doing all right, isn't he?'

'He's a bishop and a pawn up, and it's one of the oddest games I've ever seen.' I whispered.

'He's winning, though, isn't he?' whispered Speedfall back, anxiously.

'I suppose so,' I said, doubtfully.

Speedfall looked thoughtful.

'I'd better get him some more beer,' he decided.

Bronson seemed intrigued by Robinson's latest move.
Had he not realised that pawns could, if they wished, move
one square at a time? He seemed resolved to try the move
out for himself: Pawn to Queen's Knight Three.

Where was Robinson now going to swoop? The field
seemed wide open.

I suppose he thought that even against such an obvious
idiot as his opponent seemed to be, some sort of preparation
was needed for a breakthrough in the centre. He moved
Queen to Knight's Three.

Bronson eagerly took his cue from this, and moved his
Queen to Bishop's Three. Robinson, looking distinctly ill,
as though the claret inside him had just fool's-mated
the beer, took the Queen's pawn with his Queen. He must
have reckoned doubtfully that if his opponent captured his
bishop he had a likely mate in sight by bringing up the

black bishop. Bronson's mind was elsewhere. I guessed he was feeling that he wouldn't mind tightening up the Suitcase himself. He didn't take the bishop (did he know, yet, that queens could move laterally?) but repeated with his black bishop the move he had earlier made with his white bishop, Bishop to King's Three.

It was all one to Robinson, who promptly captured the Queen's Rook.

Now came another move from Bronson which made me feel that he knew more about the game than had so far appeared. He captured Black King's Pawn. Robinson took little notice of this. He looked less like a Spanish hermit now than the corpse in Hogarth's 'Anatomy Lesson', but he pursued his Queen's rapacious adventure with a sort of listless enthusiasm. He took the knight.

'Check!' he murmured.

'Cheerio!' replied Bronson, sensing that the next piece in the path of his opponent's queen might be in some danger, and moving it out of the way (King to King Two). Robinson took the rook's pawn.

'Check!'

'Cheerio!' replied Bronson, moving the king back again.

Then Robinson made the worst move he had ever made in his life, a move he was later to blame upon the fatal conjunction of grape and grain, combined with the strong possibility of some sort of oriental hypnosis. I suppose some still-rational and unnauseated corner of his reeling brain had the notion of dislodging the white queen and joining his line of advancing pawns. It was a fatal error: Bishop's Pawn takes King's Pawn. The white queen was dislodged all right. Bronson took her by the neck as though she were the Suitcase and advanced her to Bishop's Seven.

'Cheerio!' he beamed.

And well he might say so, for it was a clear mate in two moves and Robinson immediately resigned, just in time to see Speedfall returning with his replenishment of beer. He took one look at the foaming glass, turned a pale green (greener than the Mongolians – almost as green as the Suitcase's hair) and fled from the room.

The Suitcase, clearly delighted that her rival for Fergus's company had been put down, gave a little scream of pleasure and clapped her hands. The Mongolians stood up at this, as though at a signal. Bronson was already triumphantly on his feet, running his tongue over his lips. He put out his hand in such a way that if Robinson had still been in the room he might have expected him to shake it. As it was, the Suitcase looked as though she thought it might be reaching for one of her zips or padlocks. Fergus had already made a move to follow his defeated friend, and she needed no inducement to follow. And as they left, the Mongolians left, grinning and chattering, with lecherous haste.

Speedfall was appalled. He looked so disconsolate, standing there with Robinson's beer as the room emptied, that I felt I had to cheer him up.

'Don't worry,' I said. 'I'm sure your Uncle Jeremy wouldn't have actually wanted us to beat them, would he?'

He was forced to agree with that, and when it became clear that the rest of the ad hoc College chess team was positively glad to be relieved of their duties, bidding him eager farewells and guarded thanks for the evening's entertainment, he brightened up considerably.

'You're right,' he said. 'But what are they up to now? Where on earth have they gone?' Sounds of Bacchanalian pursuit and ineffective protest came distantly from the Cloisters and were to recur through the night in strange parts of the College.

We never discovered the answer to Speedfall's questions, but from information which privately reached the Dean the following morning and from the dark hints and veiled accusations which he consequently threw in Speedfall's direction, it was plain that Robinson's amnesty was not only considered a mistake, never to be repeated, but that he and his friends might well have been forbidden the College for all time if it had not been for the role played by Speedfall's guests, whom Robinson claimed to be the real culprits.

'They enjoyed themselves, at all events,' I remarked to Speedfall some days later, encountering him in the Lodge.

'So I am led to understand,' said Speedfall, waving a letter that had arrived that morning from his Uncle Jeremy.

'You know,' I added cautiously, not sure how far Speedfall had taken in the Mongolians' obsession, 'I do believe they thought that punk girl was a boy.'

Speedfall was absorbed in his letter.

'You do?' he said absently.

'The green hair probably did it. Like the green carnation. They kept asking about Oscar Wilde.'

Speedfall didn't seem to be listening. I went on:

'And I'm willing to bet that far from being a chess team, they'd never played chess before in their lives.'

Speedfall looked up seriously at that.

'Do you know,' he said. 'It's a most extraordinary thing, but you're absolutely right. My uncle apologises. Says he hopes we didn't find them difficult, but he was doing a favour for the Minister of Sport, who's a particular friend of his. They're a gymnastics team.'

'There you are,' I said. 'It explains everything.'

Speedfall finished his letter and looked at me in despair.

'And they're in the process of defecting to the West. They like it here.'

'Oh no,' I said.

Gaudy Gaudy Gumdrops

The college was looking at its best when the old members began to arrive for the gaudy. It was a sunny day in late June, the sky a clear blue except for a few tight scrolls of white cloud bunched up as high as you could imagine, clean and still as though they had nothing at all to do with the weather. Birds carolled their welcome to the BMWs, Volvos, Porsches and occasional dented Fords that nosed their way into the car park, and the roses ever so slightly unfolded to release their scent as the old members entered the front quad with their overnight suitcases.

In the Lodge, Marshal was in his element.

'Thank you, Mr Dacres. Don't forget your key . . . Mr Matchbody, isn't it? I'm absolutely well, sir, thank you . . . Good afternoon, Mr Watcher . . . Mr Rumpard? Yes, I thought it was you. Your brother still out in Kenya? . . . Here you are, Mr Köthner, I've put you in your old room, Back Quad III . . . Thank you, sir, and the same to you.'

As each old member departed to unpack and to stroll through the college, renewing memories and old acquaintances, Marshal delivered to Stores, his young underporter, brief biographies of the former undergraduates. His tone was fond, admiring, wistful. This was a breed of hero never to come again, he implied. The undergraduates of today were lesser men, and (the inference was inevitable) needed only inferior porters like Stores to look after them.

'Mr Dacres is in the Foreign Office. Mr Spelsbury is Member of Parliament for Duffington East. Mr Clark (that's P. P. Clark, not Clarke, R.N., with an e) was in Canada for a number of years. He's doing very well now, I believe. Ever such a shy lad when he first came up.'

Stores nodded, in glazed boredom.

'Mr Harness is coming. Now his father was here, and his grandfather. You read about him the other day in the papers, I expect. In the financial pages. Now see who's coming. This one's a laugh, I can tell you. Good afternoon, Mr Gracego!'

Like the others, Herbert Gracego collected his key and exchanged pleasantries with the porter. Most of the guests had been ticked off on the list by now and Marshal was in a tranquil mood.

'He was a caution, that Mr Gracego,' he said to the underporter. 'Always short of money. Always on the scrounge. You should have seen him with the OUDS, though. Marvellous actor. Of course, you'll have watched him on the telly. That commercial, you know, the one for the sherry. What is it? "Dry as his sermon!" Ah, hello, Mr Watkins. Just in time for the Principal's tea, are we?'

Mr Watkins was indeed in time for the Principal's tea. I was there myself, as a matter of fact, along with a few other invited Fellows, to meet a generation of undergraduates in many cases only dimly remembered, to drink Earl Grey tea and eat egg-and-cress sandwiches the size of Tanna Touva postage stamps, and wish I were doing something else.

'Better not eat too many of these,' smiled a portly old member on my left. 'I'm thinking of what's to come.'

'Yes, indeed,' I replied. 'And the chef's in rather good form these days.'

The portly old member nodded briefly as if he took all that for granted (and indeed the dinner itself was without question the main attraction of the weekend). He continued to look at me, twinkling with amusement.

'You don't remember me, do you?' he said.

Agonies, I thought. It always happens. Someone I've forgotten. This was the second or third generation of undergraduates I had taught at Oxford, men now in their late thirties at least, well beyond the malleable freshness of their youth and into the practised disguises of their successful middle age, wearing their paunches and incipient baldness like trophies. I had to confess I was beaten.

'Jerry Rumpard!' he exclaimed, with an air of modest pride in the mere syllables of his name. People always betray themselves when pronouncing their own names. He uttered his with a quiet relish that was like the aural equivalent of incised brass. 'Jerry Rumpard.' I could see it on letterheads, on memoranda.

'Of course,' I said, unconvincingly.

'I changed to German after two terms,' he reminded me. 'I'm with Laggard's now and it's not been a bit of use. All that Heine.'

'Ah yes,' I said. 'I don't think you were interested in my subject either, were you?'

'You scared me to death, actually,' said Rumpard, biting into another sandwich. Since they were so small, however, biting into them was more like biting around them. The whole object was popped into his large mouth, and the pink jaw flexed for a moment before he swallowed.

Rumpard, as if pitying my feeble memory, became my unofficial interpreter for the occasion.

'You remember George du Marque, I suppose?' he would hiss, as some gaunt captain of industry drifted near. 'In the process of ruining Venezuelan Zinc.'

I didn't bother to move away. Rumpard was happy to talk and didn't expect much comment from me.

'P. P. Clark,' he murmured. 'Into his third wife. Oh, and over in the corner that's Bertie Gracego. Remember the skeleton in the Dean's pew at Evensong after Torpids?'

I remembered.

'He was on that dreadful quiz programme. Haven't heard much of him recently, though. Looks a bit foul-tempered, doesn't he?'

Gracego was indeed skulking by himself in a gloomy trance. I remembered him as a brilliant mimic in the ETC revue, and something of a pianist. He wasn't exactly the life and soul of the party now.

'Is Mesborough coming?' I asked, thinking of another bright spark of those days.

'Dead,' said Rumpard.

'Oh dear.'

'Went a bit pious, I think, and was mugged or something, somewhere in the Far East.'

'That's a pity.'

'It comes to us all,' said Rumpard, looking for the tray of cream cakes.

I know what's coming to you, I thought to myself. The chairmanship of Laggard's and a coronary before you're sixty. Or perhaps you'll survive and strike out cheerfully on your own. Laggard's. Rumpard's. It's all one.

We ambled across the room and heard the Principal

telling a cluster of old members all the latest College news, in particular about the recent discovery of a cache of seventeenth-century silver.

'. . . dented and scratched, of course,' he was saying. 'We'll have to have it seen to before we can properly display it. Meanwhile it's safely locked in the old muniment room in the bell-tower.'

He sipped his tea.

'I shouldn't have revealed its whereabouts, I suppose,' he added sheepishly, 'but we're all friends here. I can trust you all not to talk to the press.'

There were murmurs of 'Of course, Principal' and other conspiratorial gestures. Mature faces encircled him with mock eagerness, like sycophantic schoolboys on a scouting expedition.

'Anyway,' Principal Crocusby continued, 'I shall have more to say about all these things at dinner. I really don't want to preempt my speech. Just let me say this: when we do display the silver it will be quite an occasion, I can tell you. And it will coincide with our Appeal.'

At the mention of the Appeal many of the old members gazed down with sudden interest at their toe-caps. Beyond the little group but surely within its hearing there came a subdued snort. I tried to see who had delivered this snort, and in what spirit (probably derisive, I thought), but could only see a scout collecting teacups, the Bursar talking to a silent Indian, and Gracego inspecting the curtains.

The Principal ignored the interruptions, spoke for a few moments with immensely ceremonious enthusiasm about the proposed residential block that would (unfortunately, but necessarily) overlook the Warden of Wadham's garden, and then with a smile moved away among his other guests.

But many had already disappeared, perhaps to take a stroll in the gardens before Chapel, or to run a bath before changing for dinner, or simply to find a moment somewhere alone where they could try to imagine what they had been like twenty years before and to wonder if they too, like those they saw all around them, still preserved within their thickening frame the ghost of the departed Adonis.

I skipped Chapel, and survived sherry on the lawn of Back Quad in the company of some former pupils that I did happen to remember, men like Roddy Santa Cruz and Charlie Harness, both now teaching in London schools, and Bill Smith, editor at one of the big paperback houses. The latter asked me, as he always did when we met, if my book on Laforgue was ready yet.

'Not yet, I'm afraid.'

'Let me know when it is.'

'Why? Would you want to publish it?'

'Doubt it.'

'Why ask, then?'

We had had this conversation at least twice before in the last ten years. It had become the equivalent of saying: 'Hello, how are you?'

After ten minutes of this sort of thing I was buttonholed by Speedfall, who was moving about the lawn spreading alarm and despondency.

'The Principal is being very indiscreet,' he hissed.

'How?' I asked.

'He's going on and on about the silver.'

'Well?'

'It's not insured yet, and it was agreed on the Bursarial Committee to keep quiet about it until the Appeal.'

I shrugged.

'Well, it's too late now,' I replied. 'I don't see what harm can be done.'

'You know quite well what harm can be done,' retorted Speedfall. 'We'll have the whole of Fleet Street on our necks. What's more, he's been telling everyone how much it will cost to restore it.'

'Oh dear,' I said.

'Yes,' insisted Speedfall. 'It's highly counterproductive at this stage. Besides, I really don't think it's at all safe in the Muniment Tower. Suppose it gets stolen?'

'I'm afraid Maurice can't usually be stopped from doing things his own way.'

'Maurice,' snapped Speedfall, pronouncing the Principal's first name as though it were itself a prime example of its owner's incompetence, 'ought to take some leave.'

'Heads of houses don't get leave,' I said.

'There'll be a statute somewhere,' smiled Speedfall grimly. 'You'll be sure I'll find it.'

I did rather agree with Speedfall as a matter of fact. The silver, hoarded for safety at the time of the Civil War to save it from being cut up and stamped for soldiers' pay, was far less safe than it had ever been. As far as I knew it was simply in an old cupboard. Some of it was even lying on the archivist's desk. And the College was always having things stolen.

But our conversation had to end there, as the Butler was calling us into Hall for dinner. As we shuffled up the steps in our black gowns like a hundred or so ravens, a couple of real ravens flew above and fluttered for a moment at a lewd gargoyle over our heads.

'Ah,' said the Dean, just behind us. 'The temple-haunting martlet.'

The words seemed curiously doom-laden and prophetic.

A couple of hours later the noise and temperature in Hall were about the equivalent of those in the furnace of a steel-works. We were on to our fifth wine-glass, our faces rubicund, bow-ties askew, chattering inconsequentially.

'What's this?' exclaimed Charlie Harness, as yet another plate was put in front of him. 'I've already eaten more than I usually eat in a week.'

'Angels on horseback,' said someone.

'Which is the angel and which is the horse?' asked Charlie, pushing the prune out of his roll of bacon with a fork.

'It's devils on horseback,' said someone else.

A little farther down the table Jerry Rumpard looked up mournfully.

'It should be an oyster, not a prune,' he complained.

'That's angels,' said someone.

'Devils,' said someone else.

I thought that the devils seemed much more appropriate, given the cavernous blackness of the Hall with its multitudes of dark shapes only fitfully lit by the smoky candles. The sort of scene that Milton must have known at Christ's:

> . . . the spacious hall,
> Though like a covered field, where champions bold
> Wont ride in armed, and at the Soldan's chair
> Defied the best of Panim chivalry
> To mortal combat or career with lance
> Thick swarmed, both on the ground and in the air,
> Brushed with the hiss of rustling wings . . .

After a meal such as we had eaten, this lot might feel like champions but they looked pretty vanquished to me. I doubt they could even have construed Milton ('Won't ride in armed' what . . . and why not?) but still, they did look like insects. I ventured the likeness to Ted Wigan who was sitting just across from me.

'Don't read Milton,' he said shortly, sipping a glass of water.

My heart sank. I had forgotten how dangerous it was to talk shop with a modernist (or was he a post-modernist?) Marxist (post-Marxist?) English tutor.

'Do you mean I shouldn't, or you don't?' I asked, realising that I sounded far more belligerent than I had intended.

'Do what you like,' he said. 'Milton betrayed the Revolution.'

'What do you mean?'

'Scared stiff when it looked like really taking off. Back-pedalled. An authoritarian.' Wigan glowered at me.

'I see,' I said. 'Do you teach Milton?'

'Teach?' snapped Wigan with a bitter laugh. 'Teach? What's that?'

One of the old members who had read English and were seated around Wigan in the vain hope that they might have something in common, spoke up timidly.

'We were taught Milton by Friendish, of course. He always gave tutorials in his pyjamas.'

'Friendish!' exclaimed Wigan. His lips struggled to form some kind of smile. 'Friendish liked to think that Milton was an Anglican.'

Friendish would also have known the difference between angels — and devils — on horseback, I reflected. Autres temps, autres moeurs.

The main part of dinner was concluded, and the Principal rose from his Soldan's chair to say grace. Benches scraped, a few glasses were knocked over, and there was much hissing of rustling wings. Everyone sat down again, and a murmur broke out compounded of prandial relief, polite attention to neglected neighbours and mild interest in speeches and other future entertainment.

The Principal explained the procedure that was to follow, although, like every other aspect of the gaudy, it had already been elaborately explained beforehand. In Hall the Principal presided as head of the College. In Common Room he did not so preside. Common Room was entirely in the hands of the Vice-Principal who presided there in temporary seniority to the Principal. The Principal, in effect, partook of Common Room as a guest of the Common Room, and on ordinary evenings when the Fellows repaired from Hall to the actual Common Room, clutching their napkins, he would signify his relinquishing of authority by bowing to the Vice-Principal at the door. The Vice-Principal would return his bow and lead the way in to fruit, nuts, snuff and port.

This evening, dessert would be served in Hall. After grace, the Principal would leave, followed by the Vice-Principal. Then the Vice-Principal would return, followed by the Principal, and the gathering would be deemed to have reconstituted itself into a Common Room.

Having explained all this, the Principal left the Hall. And so too did the Vice-Principal, to much general merriment. The tables were cleared for dessert, and many of the guests took the opportunity to slip away to the lavatory. Some of the Fellows changed places with each other at this point, either to give the old members a change of face or to escape from their attentions. Speedfall ousted Ted Wigan (who seemed to leave for good) and leaned across to me.

'Now for the speeches,' he whispered. 'I hope that Maurice knows what he's doing.'

'I expect he does,' I said.

'He hasn't been looking himself recently,' said Speedfall. 'I hope he doesn't go on about the silver.'

'There's not much that we can do about it, anyway,' I pointed out.

I turned to chat with Charlie Harness, mainly, I must admit, to prevent him from lighting up before the Queen. I was too cowardly actually to mention the prohibition, even though he had a Dunhill in one hand and was flicking a lighter with the other.

Just then we noticed the Vice-Principal going up to the High Table, turning round, looking puzzled, and then going out again.

'Oops,' said Rumpard. 'Forgotten something?'

'Where's the Principal, then?' asked Roddy Santa Cruz.

'Had a little too much and gone back to the Lodgings,' said someone farther down the table. Someone else laughed.

As the situation became generally understood, an amused murmur broke out round the Hall. Some moments later the Vice-Principal returned and spoke to the Dean. Speedfall, who could not bear not to know what was going on, went across to the Dean's table too.

'Can I smoke?' asked Rumpard, pulling out a large cigar.

'Not yet,' I pleaded.

'Well, I wish they'd get on with it.'

'Yes,' said Bill Smith. 'When are we going to have the loyal toast?'

'Very soon,' I said. 'When the Principal returns.'

'I hope it's soon,' said Rumpard. 'I see that quite a few sensible people have nipped out for a fag.'

Charlie Harness was well alight already, puffing smoke benevolently in all directions.

Speedfall returned to our table.

'I knew something was wrong with him,' he said. 'The Principal has disappeared.'

'What on earth do you mean?'

'He can't be found.'

'Why not? Wasn't the Vice-Principal with him?'

Speedfall shrugged.

'It's not clear at all. I think the V-P has had quite a bit of the harry lifters tonight and he's not making much sense. He says he believed that Maurice was behind him when he came back into Hall, but that he hadn't really taken much notice.'

'Has the Butler seen him? Or any of the kitchen staff?'

'The Dean has gone to investigate, but I can't think that they'll be much help either. They'll be well into the heeltaps by now.'

'What's going to happen?'

'Your guess is as good as mine.'

By this time a good deal of smoking was going on and the absence of the Principal was being generally tolerated. Dessert provided a distraction: there was even the odd bit of undergraduate-style grape-throwing. But at the same time there was a distinct undercurrent of speculation and expectation. The problem would have to be solved by the Vice-Principal, clearly. But whether he was in a fit state to do the right thing was much less clear. For a while he sat bemused in the Dean's place. Then he followed the Dean out of the Hall again. Then he returned, shortly followed by the Dean. It all seemed vaguely choreographed, like a comic demonstration of some logical paradox.

It was my opinion that the Vice-President should propose the toast of Church and Queen, explain what had happened and leave it at that. The old member who was to have proposed the health of the Principal would, I was convinced, be relieved not to have to make his speech. He was, by tradition, an ex-President of the JCR, this year more ingratiating and dull than usual, a sort of inferior Rumpard. He had been shuffling his notes nervously since the pudding course. Why not let him off the hook?

Speedfall shook his head. It wasn't only the Principal's health that was to be proposed, he pointed out. It was also the College, even primarily the College, that was to be toasted. The speech was in effect a speech of gratitude to the College by the representative of the former members gathered together here. It was, in Speedfall's view, the high point of the gaudy.

'Gaudeamus igitur,' he explained. 'How do we know they are rejoicing if he doesn't get up and say so?'

At that moment something like a walnut hit me on the left ear.

'I should have thought it went without saying, wouldn't you?' I replied. 'And won't it all be a little pointless if the Principal isn't here to respond?'

'Pointless?' said Speedfall. 'No, no. You've missed the point. The Vice-Principal must speak in reply. That's just the sort of thing we have a Vice-Principal for.'

I looked across at the doomed gentleman in question, who was polishing his glasses.

'Well, I think it's asking rather a lot of him. At the moment he doesn't look as though he could even find his way to the Founder's Box, let alone extemporise a review of the year's events.'

I should explain that it was one of the traditions of St Patrick's that whenever the Principal addressed the assembled college he should do so from a sort of ancient wooden pulpit set into the rear wall of the Hall high up in the minstrel's gallery. The point of this was not at all clear, nor were any of the words spoken from it, since its distance and confined position made the Principal's speeches barely audible. It had its own little staircase, however, running from the Buttery with worn stone steps ascending a narrow turret, the charm of which had always just failed to prevent the tradition being abandoned. Besides, on very important occasions such as a gaudy, a rudimentary sort of public address system was installed by the Bursar. Making a speech from it was, therefore, a very different matter from simply standing up at High Table, and I doubted that the Vice-Principal would be capable of it at the best of times.

Well, the decision wasn't up to either Speedfall or myself. And indeed the decision was there and then taken out of the Vice-Principal's hands, as well: as Speedfall and I were arguing sotto voce across the table the Hall suddenly fell partially silent and I saw that some people were looking up. Something was going on at the back of the Hall: it was the Principal, speaking from the Founder's Box!

He shouldn't have gone up there yet, of course, as the ex-President of the JCR had not made his speech. It was all very peculiar. Speedfall looked thunderstruck, and I could guess what he was thinking. Was Maurice really not quite himself? Where had he been? Was he going to be embarrassingly indiscreet?

In general, I suppose there was a ready acceptance of what might after all have been some official change of plan. Perhaps some of the diners didn't realise that anything much was amiss, except that the Principal had forgotten to switch on either the public address system or the little reading lamp that was provided above the lectern. As a result, his figure in the Founder's Box was dark and indistinct. Little could be seen of him except the hawk-like nose and couch-grass eyebrows, ready symbols of his imposing presence.

Speedfall needn't have worried. There were no indiscreet revelations about the silver, or about anything else, for his voice could only be intermittently heard at all. Much of what he appeared to be saying was concerned, as was customary, with the most famous of the generation of old members assembled – though instead of the usual platitudes and pious memories (the overfamiliar rehearsal of commonplace college gossip as it might reach the ears of the Fellowship) there were some distinctly outré anecdotes and references. Most of the pay-off lines were lost, but even so there were some guffaws from the body of the Hall and one or two raised eyebrows. Attention, which would normally have been only lightly given or have wandered under the benign influence of port, was wholly given over to the largely inaudible scandal that drifted down from the dim figure in the Founder's Box. After a short while it suddenly became clear that the Principal had changed tack, and was making some extraordinary remarks about the privileged life of the cloister relative to worldly success (or the lack of it) of this graduate vintage.

'A trifle undiplomatic of the old boy,' said someone a few places away from me (I think it was Watkins). 'I'm being made redundant next month.'

'Bound to get a sermon with the fatted calf,' remarked Rumpard through his cigar.

'Sssh,' hissed Bill Smith. 'I can't hear.'

But there was nothing more to hear, for with his characteristic gesture of dismissal, raising his eyebrows and pinching the bridge of his nose, the Principal then disappeared from the Founder's Box. There was applause, but there were also a number of ironic hoots and an immediate buzz of conversation.

It was an odd performance, like a caricature of himself but strangely parsonical, as Rumpard had suggested. And we had still had no loyal toast, nor, more crucially, was it at all clear what the ex-President of the JCR was meant to do. He was flipping the notes for his speech between his fingers in an anguish of regret and hope, as though they were a bust five-card trick at pontoon. But everyone had forgotten about him.

As I left the Hall in the company of Speedfall, I suggested that surprising though the Principal's behaviour had been, it was relatively harmless: 'He may have offended some of them by his remarks about protected employment (what on earth did he mean by it?) but at least he didn't mention the silver.'

Speedfall brooded as we crossed the Back Quad arch on our way to the Beaumont Room for coffee.

'That's just it. That's what worries me most,' he said.

'What do you mean?'

'I'm worried that he didn't talk about the silver.'

'I would have thought you would have been relieved.'

'In a way,' replied Speedfall. 'But don't you see: he's been talking about the silver all day, and threatening to talk about it tonight, too. It's on his mind. He sees it as a symbol of the restored fortunes of the College, and feels personally responsible for its discovery. Why should he suddenly appear to forget all about it? Why should he go off like that, and then make such mayhem of the usual arrangement of the speeches? Why make such a smug, such a comically smug, speech himself? He sounded as though he were imitating the Dean. And what's more, where is he now?'

I couldn't really disagree with any of this. For once it seemed that Speedfall was right, and that there was something wrong with Maurice. And indeed he seemed to have disappeared again – unless he had returned to the Lodgings, which would at the least have been somewhat antisocial of him.

It was a beautiful evening, and a group of Fellows had gathered on the lawn to look at the night sky. I'm hopeless when it comes to stars. I could just about make out Ursa Major and Ursa Minor circling each other like wary tadpoles, but the finer points of the conversation escaped me. I could find Arcturus easily enough, but Boötes himself was a mystery.

'That's his foot, below Arcturus,' explained Curidge. 'Surely you can see that?'

Yes, I could see the foot all right, but I couldn't see the rest of him. And who had first identified that constellation as a herdsman, and why, and why was he herding bears, of all things? Curidge patiently had to explain.

'What you are referring to as Ursa Major is only part of it,' he said, as though talking to a ten year-old. 'What you are looking at is the Big Dipper, a modern asterism of course.'

'Of course,' I said.

'And as for Boötes,' he began. I didn't really hear what he said because I was distracted by the College bells which had started to ring. You may think that the ringing of the College bells on the night of a gaudy was the most natural thing in the world, a cheerful proclaimer of festivity and general glee. Well, in the ordinary course of events it would have been, though in fact we never had the bells rung at that hour. But it happened that recently some fine cracks had been discovered in two of the oldest bells. These bells were known as Old Mick and Young Nick, though both dated from the early sixteenth century, being a direct bequest from the Founder, transferred at that time from Llanbadrig in North Wales – one of the most tangible links between St Patrick's and its Founder, not lightly to be allowed to fall into disrepair. I knew about the state of the bells because I happened to be on the Chapel Committee, where it had been agreed that the bells should not be rung until they had been inspected and the College been given an expert opinion. The matter had not yet come to the Governing Body, so that most of the Fellows thought little of the sound of the bells, being too deep in port and Boötes to give them a second thought.

Speedfall and I exchanged glances. He was also on the Chapel Committee, and was obviously thinking what I was thinking. Even as we looked at each other I could see that it suddenly occurred to him, as it occurred to me, that this odd event might have some connection with the main odd event of the evening. It was only a flash of intuition, and I don't think either of us had any idea of what the connection might be, but we were both thinking it, I could tell.

Curidge was now talking about Hercules and the way he appears to be shooting at Cygnus:

'. . . perhaps representing the Stymphalian Birds, one of the Herculean Labours . . .' he droned. Speedfall and I moved away from the group.

'I think we should go and see why the bells are being rung,' I said. 'They shouldn't be, should they?'

'Indeed not,' he said. 'And what's more they're making a very inexpert sound, aren't they?'

It was true. They hadn't been sounding for more than perhaps a minute, but already they were carelessly out of coordination, sounding more like a jangle than a peal. We hastened through to the Front Quad, passing Rumpard and one or two others who were strolling with linked arms and singing ditties in falsetto voices.

'Don't think much of your bell-ringers,' he called out genially as we passed. 'They sound as pissed as we are.'

We simply smiled apologetically and went on. No need to cause a general alarm. We found the door to the bell tower locked and the sounds coming from it stranger than ever, random, intermittent, mistimed. After a moment they stopped.

'What on earth's going on in there?' cried Speedfall. 'Is it some sort of a joke?'

'We'd better go to the Lodge,' I suggested.

We met the Dean at the Lodge, and he knew no more about the bells than we did. Marshal had gone home, and so had the young underporter who had been on duty with him that day. We found only the night porter, an old part-timer called Snile, who was eating an enormous bacon sandwich and clearly didn't like being disturbed.

'I've been trying to get to this sandwich for quarter of an hour,' he complained. 'It's all cold now.'

'Your sandwich is the least of our worries, I'm afraid,'

74

said Speedfall politely. 'Can we have the key to the bell tower please?'

'Cor stone the crows,' said Snile. 'Again? I've just given out the key to the bell tower, not five minutes ago.'

'I imagine you must have done, judging by that racket,' said the Dean. 'Who did you give it to? You ought to know very well that the tower key is not to be given out to anyone except on my authority or the Principal's, particularly in view of the need for the special security of the muniment room. It's most irresponsible of you.'

Snile bridled.

'There's no need to take that attitude, sir, I can assure you. It was the Principal himself who asked for it. All proper and above board.'

Seeing the consternation on our faces, he smiled the faintest of self-satisfied smiles and ventured to take a large bite of his sandwich, looking at us mischievously over the top of his thick spectacles.

'The Principal!' exclaimed Speedfall, aghast.

'You'd better give us the spare key to the tower, Snile,' said the Dean grimly.

'Right you are, sir,' said the porter, moving very slowly to the rack of keys and taking one down. 'Sign here please.'

'I don't need to sign for it, Snile. I'm the Dean.'

'I know that, sir,' said Snile. 'It's your own rule. Everyone has to sign. The Principal signed. Very readily, if I may say so.'

Speedfall took the porter's book.

'Let's see that signature,' he said. 'I thought as much. The Principal's quite off his rocker. Look.'

We looked at the signature in the key-book. It read: 'Gaudy gaudy gumdrops, with love from Dracula.'

'Didn't you see this, man?' rapped the Dean, thrusting the offending words before Snile's nose.

'I'm sorry, sir,' said Snile. 'I can't see a thing in these glasses.'

'It's no use staying here arguing,' said Speedfall. 'We must go back to the tower. The Principal has locked himself in there, and who knows what may be happening. Should we ring for a doctor?'

'Let's just go and see first, shall we?' I said.

When we entered the bell tower we found it locked with the first key from the inside as we expected. On the stone floor beneath the bells lay the Principal, stretched out on his back as though asleep, with one arm flung out and the other twisted beneath him. The bell-ropes were still swinging slightly, and the end of one was caught around his foot.

You may imagine our consternation and alarm at the sight. There was no movement, no pulse. The Principal had had some sort of fatal seizure.

We naturally rang for an ambulance, and fetched Curidge, who as Tutor in Physiology might be expected to confirm the diagnosis and to suggest what we might do if we happened to be mistaken. Alas, we were not mistaken. As Curidge bent over the body, delicately touching its vital junctions and signals, we could tell that he found no sign of life.

'We shall have to ring his sister,' said Speedfall. 'What can we say to her? And the press: how can we explain? We can't let it be known that the Principal had a brainstorm like this.'

'I don't see how we can prevent it,' said the Dean.

'It won't do the College any good,' went on Speedfall,

half to himself. 'It's just the sort of thing that the news-papers like to get their teeth into.'

'Well, it hasn't done the Principal any good,' I reflected. 'It's poor Maurice we should be thinking about, isn't it?'

'Quite right,' said the Dean. 'And in any case I'm sure we can keep the details to ourselves. That message in the key-book, for a start.'

As Curidge straightened up from his examination of the body we turned to him expectantly.

'He's dead all right,' he confirmed. 'But I doubt we can keep the details from the press. Not any of them.'

'Why not?' asked Speedfall.

'Because it wasn't a seizure,' said Curidge. 'The skull is badly cracked. And also because it isn't Maurice. This is the body of a much younger man. Look.'

Even as he turned the face towards us in that dim light I suddenly saw that of course he was right. The neck and jaw in particular were quite different.

'I think this is what fooled us,' said Curidge, unhooking the nose. It came away in his fingers, a thin jelly-like structure. The bushy eyebrows came off, too. There were pads in the cheeks and a towel inside the shoulders of the dinner jacket to make the frame bulkier. With all these removed it was quite easy to see that the body was not that of the Principal.

'Good Lord,' I exclaimed. 'It's Bertie Gracego.'

'Quite a brilliant imitation, don't you think?' said Curidge. 'It must have taken some planning.'

'What was it all for?' I asked.

The answer was not long to find. Curidge had lifted up the body in order to remove the disguise. Beneath it lay a circular metal object engraved with the College crest and a Latin inscription. Similar articles were found in the pockets.

'I knew it,' said Speedfall. 'I knew something like this would happen.'

It was the College silver.

That was it, of course. A somewhat elaborate attempt to steal something not only valuable in itself (though surely not easily marketable) but a symbol of all that poor Gracego had presumably come to hate in his old college: style, tradition, continuity, certainty of wealth. For it turned out that he had failed in his acting career and had really had no steady employment for years, despite a mild comic notoriety among his contemporaries almost entirely due to that television sherry advertisement which had contributed to the manner of his delivery of the Principal's speech. Climbing the bell-ropes to get at the silver must have been an extemporisation (a small window looked out from the muniment room on to the bells themselves). How much of the theft was an inspired afterthought due to the Principal's indiscretions at tea we never discovered. The Principal himself, locked in a pantry, was unharmed. The details were kept from the police, and the coroner was therefore persuaded that the whole business was simply the result of a drunken spree. Perhaps it was only that, a theatrical gesture of a sort, a kind of protest.

'Why do we do it?' I asked Speedfall. 'Why do we all pretend that all our graduates are happy and successful – and rich?'

'Most of them are,' he said.

'Not Gracego,' I said. 'He was out of work and lumbered with friends and traditions and a way of life that required an income he had never managed to obtain. Why should he rejoice in his rich old college?'

'Not the College's fault,' said Speedfall. 'Though Maurice rather had what was coming to him.'

It made me wonder what might, in due course, be coming to the College. What would happen when the mighty empires of Laggard's and Rumpard's and the rest of them foundered? What ghosts would come home to roost then?

It gave me a cold feeling down my back.

The Lodge was collectively appalled and delighted by what had happened. 'That Mr Gracego,' said Marshal. 'You've got to hand it to him, haven't you?'

'How was I to know?' Snile said. 'He were a dead ringer for the Principal.'

Marshal laughed.

'Yes,' he said. 'And he was a dead ringer on his own account.'

A Mushroom Mystery

When old Hapwool heard that I had planned a tour in North Wales he was most insistent that I should call and see him. When I added that I was taking Speedfall along too he was (very politely) just a little less insistent. A sort of shadow crossed his face. Speedfall has that effect on people, and we are all used to it at St Patrick's. Even his students, in their particularly inventive sort of tolerance, had managed to make a virtue out of the effect – even in a sense to be proud of it. Theirs was the most creatively obtuse, the most intrepidly clumsy, the most determinedly interfering of tutors. There was nothing they could do about it and it was worth a fond boast or two. In Hapwool, it produced a momentary freezing of his cheery old smile.

'Drop in at any time, both of you,' Hapwool had said. 'Paula and I would be delighted to see you.'

'Well,' I had replied, 'I don't know that we shall be in your part. The Lleyn Peninsula's a bit out of our way. We're looking at castles.'

'Oh, we've a few of those,' was his reply.

I made some demur. The truth is that although I had always liked Brian Hapwool himself, I couldn't stand his wife. He was a retired botanist (a mycologist of some distinction) and an Emeritus Fellow of the College. Within the space of a few years he had married one of the departmental secretaries, taken early retirement and gone off to one of the College's cottages in the parish of Llanbadrig to eat hallucinogenic mushrooms. For a time, if you remember, they were all the rage. You could almost have said the same of Paula Hapwool, who used to be seen at all the smartest undergraduate parties before her marriage, and was the subject of some racy innuendoes in *Cherwell*'s gossip column. Come to think of it, she used to be seen at the smartest undergraduate parties after her marriage, too, and that was part of what I didn't like about her.

On the other hand, Speedfall seemed actually tolerant of her. Perhaps because she once listened for at least ten minutes, with wide eyes and a serious nodding face, to a series of celebrated Speedfallian paradoxes about why she was herself and not someone else. What he didn't see was her snorting explosion of laughter a few minutes later at the other end of the garden party, and the sycophantic drollery of some attendant twits. She had no mind to speak of, though she had plenty of the rest. Whether Speedfall was interested in the rest has always been for me a topic of unfulfilled curiosity. But no matter. He had been flattered, and that was enough for him to be ready with half-thought-out tributes to her looks and intelligence. To be ready, indeed, to find a visit to the Hapwool's cottage at Llanbadrig a not unwelcome diversion from the historical purposes of our trip.

'You will be tired of castles at some point,' he explained. 'It will be a welcome change from gwely y brecwast.'

'The Welsh do extremely good breakfasts,' I argued.

'Well, I'd like to see his mushrooms.'

'You can even get mushrooms for breakfast,' I said. 'And lamb chops.'

'No, no,' replied Speedfall. 'The other kind, that give you a glimpse of the seventh heaven. Before breakfast, too.'

'I'd never have suspected you of an interest in mind-bending drugs.'

'Well, I'm interested in the mind, anyway,' said Speedfall.

Thus it was that rather against my better judgment we made arrangements to call on Hapwool, zig-zagging awkwardly around the sprawling peaks of Snowdonia, via Beddgelert and Penygroes, in the direction of the relatively remote and smaller mountains of Llanbadrig and environs. 'Mind-bending' was a bit of an exaggeration. Hapwool was in the process of producing a new classification of the fungi of the British Isles, and found the Welsh climate stimulating. 'All that damp,' he would say. 'It sets the little buggers sprouting.' He had already located three, possibly four, new kinds of fungus – one of them apparently already sought after by a commune of druidical dropouts living in a deserted village in the area. The 'magic mushroom,' together with the robes and shaven heads of its temporary worshippers, had featured in the newspapers. You may remember reading something about it. There was an investigation of some sort by the Drugs Squad, but nothing could be proved against the offending fungus. The hallucinations were variously blamed on fraud or malnutrition, and the druids were returned to their parents' homes in Gerrards Cross and High Wycombe. Hapwool was relieved.

'Now I can get on with it in peace,' he had said. When taxed in Common Room about the reputed properties of the fungus he had merely smiled and fished out a dried sample from a little tin in his pocket, reconstituting it there and then in a glass of madeira.

'Try it, anyone?'

There were no takers. It's funny how timid some people are about these things. The fungus was a sort of rosy purple, and it bulged out of Hapwool's glass like a piece of offal. The Dean of Divinity offered to exorcise it.

I knew that Speedfall didn't care for being given strange things to eat, particularly since the episode of Manderson's wriggly porridge. I taxed him with this, as we drove through the Welsh valleys in his little tinny car. It was the sixteenth of July, a warm and sunny day.

'He doesn't just eat the things, you know,' he replied. 'I'm very interested in the principles of classification.'

It was an appropriate reason for Speedfall, as a philosopher, to give me – but as I have already suggested, I didn't think it was a wholly honest one. He looked at me sideways from the steering-wheel which he held stiffly and with an air of slight surprise, as though it were a tray of hot tea he had just tilted inwards on to his lap. He was an astonishingly dangerous driver.

'Miller is very interested in his principles of classification, too,' he said.

'Miller?'

'Miller of Merton. A rather more up-to-date mycologist than your friend Hapwool.'

'*My* friend Hapwool?' I exclaimed. 'It was you who was so keen on paying him a visit.'

'Purely out of scientific curiosity,' he said.

I pumped Speedfall about Miller and realised that I did in fact vaguely know who he was, for the chap had once been Junior Proctor. An over-vigorous Junior Proctor in my opinion, too, who did things like inspecting the Examination Schools in an 83-degree week in late June to make sure that all the candidates were still wearing jackets and gowns. I decided that on these grounds alone I did not care much for Miller. I had been content as an examiner (a mere examiner!) to admit a candidate whose white bow-tie was a simulacrum biroed on to the front of his white T-shirt. Anything for a quiet life. But Miller was a stirrer-up of trouble. What trouble might he be stirring up for Hapwool?

The first thing that emerged was that Miller had very different ideas about the properties of Hapwool's discoveries, or even as to whether they were properly discoveries at all. Two of them in particular were in question, both of them chanterelles, cousins of the little apricot-coloured trumpets that turn up in mossy walls and banks of streams in old woods (a beautiful French name I always thought, but it turns out that the French actually call them *girolles*). One of them, Miller said, *Cantharellus violaceus*, was already known, though immensely rare. This was the object which Hapwool had fished out of his waistcoat pocket one night in College, the reputed mind-bender. The other, *Cantharellus Hapwoolii*, was of a similar violet colour, but somehow different. The argument between them was of a startling simplicity. Hapwool considered *violaceus* quite harmless, just the thing for an Oxford Common Room, like an after-dinner conundrum; whereas its cousin, the variety named for him, he had termed deadly. Miller thought the *violaceus* quite dangerous, and had apparently just published a paper arguing that *Hapwoolii* was harmless. Who shall decide, when doctors disagree? I had refused Hapwool's offering in Common Room, and I certainly had no intention of trying further varieties on his home ground.

'But you see,' said Speedfall, ignoring my cowardly pro-
testations, 'the most interesting question is, what *makes* a
new variety? Miller's point is that either the terms of classification are continually modified to accommodate the
previously unknown specimen within them, or they are
rigidly adhered to, and a specimen that doesn't conform
must then be a novelty.'

It was a warm day. I was lulled by the motion of the car
and the speeding landscape, and lost the thread.

'What's that?' I muttered.

'Furthermore,' he went on. 'The new specimen throws
doubt on the classification of all the others.'

He crashed the gears and sailed out triumphantly to
overtake a lorry.

'I really don't follow you entirely,' I said.

'Just as I'm not going to follow that lorry,' he said
smugly. 'Spots. Green spots.'

'What *are* you going on about?'

'Green spots, for example. It's no good defining your new
variety by its green spots if you haven't been noticing spots at
all. You don't know whether it's new because the spots aren't
yellow, or because none of the others have spots at all.'

'Surely that would be obvious?'

'Yes, yes. It's an obvious example. But suppose I was
to substitute a more elusive characteristic. Size, let's say.
How would you decide whether a specimen was outside its
particular variety's parameter in that respect?'

'I see. You mean, when does a tall man become a giant?'

'In a way,' said Speedfall. 'Since giants are fabulous
there's no problem. A man of six feet, or six feet eleven, or
eight feet eleven for that matter, is still a man. Men aren't
defined by their height. You don't count it.'

'How do you decide what counts with mushrooms, then?'

'How indeed? That is Miller's argument. Suppose you have, after all, been noticing spots. Suppose the spots are just a bit darker yellow than usual. Are they as different (*as* spots, that is) from the usual yellow spots as, say, the green spots would be? If not, why not?'

'Why not, indeed?' I replied. 'Do look out for that car!'

Speedfall pressed his horn indignantly at the offending car.

'That is precisely what Miller argues,' he resumed. 'Hapwool is being far too free with his claims. He says that if you take Hapwool's view to its logical conclusion, you would end up with every individual becoming a species.'

'Ghastly thought,' I said.

'Hapwool, in fact,' concluded Speedfall, 'is horribly out-of-date.'

'Or horribly revolutionary.'

Speedfall shrugged.

'It amounts to the same thing,' he said. 'Philosophically speaking, he lacks elegance.'

To reach the Hapwool cottage you have to take an unlikely hidden turning out of the village of Llanbadrig, a single-track road going straight up the mountain. Speedfall overshot it, and had to reverse, with much crashing of gears and the knocking over of two dustbins. He took the road in second gear throughout, somewhat unnecessarily I thought, so that we shook and roared like a small biplane. After the first ascent, the road levelled out and followed the contours of the mountain. In the distance there was a man approaching us.

'Hadn't you better slow down a bit?' I said.

'Not much traffic on this road,' said Speedfall. 'This is

walking country. Glorious, isn't it?' He hurtled along, gravel machine-gunning the underneath of the car, brambles crowding and whipping the side windows.

'It may well be walking country, but if you don't slow down there's one walker just ahead who'll be forced to give up the activity for good.'

Speedfall slowed down.

'Perhaps he'd like a lift,' he said.

I was puzzled, but when I looked again I could see that the figure, just now on the crest of the road a few hundred yards away, was in fact walking not towards us but was travelling in the same direction. As we approached he indeed hailed us, by raising his stick. The car pulled up beside him.

'Speedfall, my dear fellow,' said the man. 'How good to see you. I'd heard you were visiting Hapwool too. Perhaps we can continue together?'

He gave me a cursory nod, in a manner that contrived to be brusque and condescending and at the same time to hint at some kind of cultural or intellectual conspiracy. It was the gesture of a man who wanted you, with the least possible effort on his part, to be on his side. I knew instinctively that I didn't want to be at all on his side. And I knew it even more so when I realised who he was. He was Miller.

What an unsuitably elegant figure he cut on the rough Welsh mountainside! He was incredibly thin, and wore green corduroys of a narrow cut. His beard was trimmed to a silky shadow and his eyes looked out appealingly from beneath a new Panama hat. This was a man conscious of his appearance, and I didn't trust him an inch.

Speedfall, however, was soon chattering happily once we had set off again, and it didn't take the two of them long to destroy Hapwool's professional character utterly. They behaved like two old maids invited to a shotgun wedding. Hapwool had achieved nothing, couldn't think, couldn't write. Moreover, it was hinted darkly, he was too old for his wife, couldn't even get the hens to lay or keep a woodburning stove alight, and had obtained the Llanbadrig cottage through some very shifty dealings with the Bursar.

I kept quiet through all this. There were cottages aplenty (Payne had one, and another had been offered to the Fellows only the previous term). I was no admirer of the vogue for self-sufficiency. I suspected that his wife liked to think that she was too young for any one man. And as for his professional competence, I was inclined to admire a man who had done as much as Hapwool had, who came out with his views, risked opinion and so on. There was something open and honest about him. There seemed little that was open about Miller. Soon we were at the cottage.

Paula Hapwool greeted us, and seemed disconcerted. Her eyes fluttered as much with nervousness as with her accustomed sexual diplomacy. She looked at us one after the other as if she didn't know quite what to say.

'You were expecting us today, I hope?' asked Speedfall.

'Oh yes,' she said brightly. 'Yes, yes, I was.'

She ushered us in with a vague sweep of one hand, the other thrust in the pocket of her skirt. Miller hung up his hat and stick, and Speedfall feigned a polite interest in a brass moulded bas-relief of Caernarfon Castle. I could see him giving it a more than cursory glance in order to say something about it. There was nothing to say about it, and the ice remained unbroken. We might have hung about for ever.

'I suppose Brian's hard at work as usual?' I said.

She seemed relieved that I had spoken.

'He always is,' she said. 'Always. But he loves it. He's in his den. I think.'

That seemed an odd thing to say, and she immediately tried to explain.

'I wasn't sure whether he'd gone out early this morning. But his den is locked. He's probably still in there from last night, and didn't hear me.'

She knew it sounded lame. It was obvious to me that she didn't really know where he was. They had probably had a quarrel and he had gone off somewhere. If I had been married to Paula Hapwool I would have wanted to go off all the time. For ever.

We stood aimlessly while she knocked on the door of his den, calling his name softly. She shrugged and smiled apologetically at us.

'He may be in the wood,' she said.

We wandered out of the cottage and looked down towards the wood. I didn't feel like pushing through the bracken to search him out there. What I felt like was a cup of tea.

'It's just not my day, is it?' she said with an exasperation that was too jolly to seem either polite or genuine. While we were outside she insisted on showing us round. There wasn't much to see. For some minutes we stood in the long barn attached to the cottage while she looked in a hay-filled manger for eggs, and three brown hens fussed round our feet. Miller fastidiously kept out of their way. Speedfall picked up an axe and swung at a log. He missed.

'No luck,' said Paula. Speedfall, thinking she was referring to his axe-stroke, swung again at the log, which bounced up and hit him on the forehead.

'Oh I say,' she said. 'Do be careful with that.'

We followed her round the cottage.

'The hens haven't settled in yet. I expect they'll lay soon.'

She plucked a grass and twisted it round her finger.

'We've got goats, too,' she went on. 'Somewhere. They eat absolutely anything.'

So do I, I thought. Such as a chocolate digestive biscuit in particular. Accompanied by a cup of tea.

It was going to be an awkward visit, I could see. Speedfall was doing his clumsy best to seem happy, enthusiastically sighting a goat in the distance which turned out to be a ram. Perhaps it was a form of flirtation. Miller, on the other hand, was churlishly silent, standing with his thumbs hooked in the back of his belt, gazing out over the valley, like an estate agent with something to hide. Paula plodded through the long grass, pulling at the grass heads with her fingers, appearing to say anything that came into her head.

From the back of the cottage you could see into some of the windows, tiny though they were. The ground rose steeply behind and these views into the cottage were like little snapshots of the odd sections of the rooms they belonged to: the corner of a rug, old bottles on a window-sill, part of a piano keyboard like a liquorice all-sort. In one of them was a patch of quarry-tiles and a man's hand.

The hand was palm uppermost, and didn't move.

Fifteen minutes later, with the aid of the axe, we had broken into Hapwool's locked den. It's surprising how difficult it is to do this. All the doors in the cottage were solid affairs in plain wood, too firm and heavy to prise open. In films, policemen do it with the heel of a boot, but I don't know how they manage it.

Hapwool was quite dead, with a large bruise on his forehead. The little window was as locked as the door had been, and all his specimens stood around him in jars of alcohol like grinning babies.

Paula Hapwool's reaction was a good deal short of hysterics. Understandably so, I felt: theirs was hardly a grand passion. Still, she made a bit of noise. Miller looked grim, as though it were a natural form of academic retribution. Speedfall however seemed almost excited.

'It's a mystery,' he whispered to me. 'It's a locked room mystery.'

Speedfall is well known for leaping to unlikely conclusions, but there was in this case something challenging and dramatic about the circumstances of poor Hapwool's death. We sat about waiting for the doctor to finish his examination, comforting Paula and drinking tea. I got my cup of tea with a vengeance. We had endless cups of tea. The trouble was that by now I could have done with something much stronger.

'How did the murderer get into the room?' hissed Speedfall to me. 'You saw the door and the windows. Where was the murder weapon? Where was the blunt instrument?'

'Don't be ridiculous,' I said. 'Who would want to murder Hapwool?'

'He's a very rich man, as a matter of fact,' said Speedfall. 'I know, because he's promised a great deal of money to the College Appeal.'

'How much?' I asked.

'A *very* great deal,' said Speedfall.

Miller came over to us from the other side of the room where he had been comforting Paula.

'I think we should look to the lady, don't you?' he said.

'Of course,' I agreed. 'How is she?'

'She's very shocked,' he said. 'Quite agitated. Perhaps the doctor can give her something when he's finished in there.'

'Is there anything we can do?'

'I don't think your whispering helps.'

We tried to comfort Paula once more, but you can't really go on saying the same thing again and again. She seemed distracted in an odd sort of way. Jumpy. For instance, she would say things like: 'Oh, there're my sunglasses,' and pick up a pair from the coffee-table and pop them on her nose, where they promptly fell forward on to the tip of her nose, making her look cruelly quizzical. She seemed quieter with Miller, so we left her once again to his care and wandered off.

'Perhaps it was an accident,' I suggested, but Speedfall was not to be put off.

'It's a classic case,' he said. 'An eccentric old millionaire, living miles from anywhere. Distraught young wife . . .'

He was clearly rewriting the whole thing as a detective story. Just because Hapwool had a few spare quid to leave to the College. I didn't bother to argue any more.

At that moment the doctor came out of the study where he had been conducting his examination. He looked at us over his spectacles as he clicked his bag shut.

'You'll be just friends of the deceased, I imagine?' he asked.

We explained that we'd arrived on a visit, and that we were former colleagues.

'Ah, well, then,' he went on. 'I can best explain to you, and you can let his daughter know in your own good time.'

We explained that Paula was his wife, and the doctor raised an eyebrow.

'Is she indeed?' he said darkly.

Speedfall, feeling that Paula's character was about to be impugned, instinctively rushed to her defence.

'She's been a great prop to him in his old age,' he said. 'Never mind her. How do you think the murderer got into that room? What struck the blow? Was it a glass paperweight?'

The doctor looked at Speedfall in amazement.

'Oh, you mean the contusion just above the right eye?' he said.

'Yes, yes.'

'I don't know what your subject is at the university,' said the doctor, 'but it can be neither physiology nor mechanics.'

Nor common sense either, he seemed to imply.

'No, no,' he continued. 'I can see that you've never even tried to hit anyone on the head hard enough to kill them.'

'Certainly not,' said Speedfall.

'Well, if you had,' said the doctor, 'you'd have soon found that hitting them an upwards blow from the front would be of very little use. Very little use indeed.'

Poor Speedfall's face fell a mile. The doctor seemed to warm to his discomfiture.

'A nasty bruise, I agree, but it was almost certainly caused by his hitting his head on the corner of the desk as he fell.'

I must say I was relieved to hear this.

'I didn't think it was likely to be murder,' I said. 'Thank goodness for that. It must have been his heart.'

'Likely to be murder?' said the doctor. 'Well now. Dr

93

Hapwool was a sensible sort of fellow, wasn't he? Not likely to make mistakes?'

'I wouldn't have said so,' I replied. 'He was an experimental scientist, after all.'

'I thought so,' said the doctor. 'Well, then, I'm afraid you may be wrong. Dr Hapwool shows every sign of having suffered acute poisoning.'

You would have thought in the circumstances that someone would have come along immediately to confine us all to the cottage and take statements. However, on hearing this news we put two and two together and told the doctor about Hapwool's fungi.

'Yes,' he said. 'I'm aware of that. There were bits of it on his desk, and I'll certainly take them away for analysis. That's why I asked if he was likely to make mistakes.'

We said yet again that we didn't think that he was likely to make mistakes.

'Well,' said the doctor. 'Whatever it is has caused gross abuse to the nervous system. There is evidence of abundant secretion of saliva, tears and nasal mucus. There would have been a gradual weakening of the pulse. I'm surprised that his wife didn't hear him and go to his assistance.'

Miller had silently appeared while we were talking.

'Mrs Hapwool has gone to bed,' he said. 'Have you got some pills or something that you can give her? And might I have a look at that fungus?'

The doctor obliged with both pills and fungus.

'Ah, yes,' said Miller, squinting at the little purple fan and twirling it slowly in his fingers. '*Cantharellus violaceus*. No wonder.'

Speedfall looked at him sharply.

'You believe it's poisonous, don't you? And Hapwool doesn't – didn't?'

'Absolutely,' breathed Miller. 'And look at the result.'

'Well, we shall see,' said the doctor. 'Don't let Mrs Hapwool take more than two of those pills this afternoon. I shall come back this evening to see how she is. I have already telephoned to make arrangements for the collection of the body. Goodbye.'

When the doctor had gone, Speedfall turned to us gravely.

'I see it all now,' he said.

'Well, I don't think I do,' I replied. 'What do you mean?'

'Suicide,' said Speedfall.

'Suicide?' I echoed.

'Yes,' said Speedfall lugubriously. 'He put himself out of his misery to avoid being a burden to his wife.'

'What misery?' I exclaimed.

'Well,' he admitted, 'perhaps I don't mean misery exactly – unless there *was* something wrong with him.'

'His doctor would presumably have known that,' I replied.

'Not necessarily,' he said. 'Anyway, look at the disparity between their ages. There was no future in it.'

'There was enough future for Hapwool, I would have thought,' I said, rather angry at this. 'Maybe not for his wife. Perhaps she poisoned him for his money?'

'You're not being serious,' said Speedfall.

'No, I'm not. But I don't think you're being serious either.'

'Did anyone look for a suicide note?'

'I don't think so.'

'There you are, then. Let's do so.'

95

Miller had apparently taken it upon himself to administer the sedative to Paula Hapwool, so Speedfall and I, feeling rather like two fifth formers prowling in the headmaster's study during prayers, poked about on Hapwool's desk for the non-existent suicide note. In the course of this fruitless quest we did however find two other items which were relevant to the mystery. The first was an offprint of the article by Miller about *Cantharellus Hapwoolii*, on which a spidery hand (presumably Hapwool's) had scrawled: 'What is the bugger up to now?'; the second was a letter to Hapwool from Miller, the upshot of which seemed to be a direct challenge to Hapwool to receive from Miller a specimen which he was to classify and then eat (or not eat) according as to whether he considered it harmless or not.

'Oh yes,' said Miller casually, when we showed him the letter. 'That seemed a perfectly reasonable offer to me. I won't bore you with the details of my argument, but the point I want in general to make is that his whole system of classification is at fault. Events seem to have proved it, don't they? You understand the issue between us, I think, Speedfall?'

'Quite,' said Speedfall.

'I'm not sure that I do,' I put in. 'Hapwool thought that *violaceus* was harmless, and *Hapwoolii* deadly. You appear to believe that the distinction between them is false in any case, and yet your published views seem simply to reverse those of Hapwool's. I don't understand it and nor apparently did Hapwool.'

I showed him what the old man had written on the offprint. Miller smiled, drawing back his glistening lips from his rows of even, clenched teeth.

'That was another kind of challenge in a way,' he said.

'You will readily appreciate that priority of characteristics is of the essence in drawing these distinctions. I would be mad to claim that there were no differences at all, but the opportunity for a little scientific irony could not be passed by lightly. I think Hapwool understood me well enough.'

'I'm glad someone can,' I said. 'So you sent him a poisoned mushroom, and now he's eaten it and died. Aren't you alarmed?'

'The fungus that I sent him was not to my mind poisonous,' retorted Miller.

'Ah,' said Speedfall. 'Then you sent him *Cantharellus Hapwoolii* . . .'

'. . . and it was the *violaceus* that was found on his desk,' I added.

Speedfall was becoming interested again.

'However,' he said triumphantly, 'Hapwool himself thought that *Hapwoolii* was poisonous, and after all he identified the thing. He should know. He'd never have eaten *Hapwoolii* unless he wanted for some reason to kill himself.'

'But he didn't eat *Hapwoolii*. No one is suggesting that he did. He ate *violaceus*.'

'Which you, Miller, claim is poisonous.'

Miller silently protested with raised forearms like a conjuror showing the audience that he has nothing up his sleeves. He wore his irritating smile that tried to look seraphic but succeeded in being simply dog-like.

'All right, then,' Speedfall corrected himself. 'Which you claim is no less harmful than *Hapwoolii*?'

'Don't you mean no *more* harmful?' I said, thoroughly confused by now. 'Miller believes *Hapwoolii* to be innocuous. That was the one you sent him, wasn't it?'

'But was it the one he *ate*?' asked Speedfall.

Miller merely smiled.

Looking back on the business later, we had to admit that we were simply going round in circles that afternoon. The one thing that was obvious was the one thing that Miller's presence made it difficult to admit, and that was that Hapwool must have known perfectly well what he was doing, and he was after all (and despite Miller's professional hostility) the expert on the subject. In the absence of a reason for killing himself, it seemed likely that Miller had managed to kill him, in a kind of insane indulgence in the final solution to academic debate. I even won Speedfall round to this argument.

'You must be right,' he admitted. 'After all, it's not unlike the execution of heretics except that nowadays there's no official way of doing it.'

'And that it's Miller that's the heretic,' I added.

'I think that his ideas are very reasonable,' said Speedfall. 'You know that.'

'Yes, and yet the man is as mad as a hatter.'

The two events that set us on the right track were the results of the post-mortem together with the tests of the fungus found on Hapwool's desk; and the production of Hapwool's diary, which had not been in his study but in his bedroom. Not that these two new pieces of evidence were not at first as contradictory as all the others. The whole business seemed to thrive on paradox.

He had been poisoned all right. There had never been much doubt about that. But the pathologist was also as sure as he could be (though not of course being a mycologist) that the noxious fungus found on Hapwool's desk (on a plate, to boot, with a small table knife and indeed a salt-cellar nearby) was ninety per cent certain to have been the cause of his death, and he was pretty sure too that it was *Cantharellus Hapwoolii*. At this there was a murmur of interest at the inquest, and even more so at the production of the diary, which, it seemed, Paula Hapwool had tried ineffectually to hide. It was a slipshod sort of diary, not consistently or fully written up, and containing mostly appointments, lists, facts, diagrams and so on, but in the space for the fifteenth of July was written quite plainly and unequivocally: 'M. proposes that the argument be settled as follows. At six o'clock precisely each of us should consume 10 gm of the variety that the *other* believes deadly. Idiot, because of course he won't do it. Luckily specimens of *viol.* and *Hap.* to hand.'

The coroner, with an air of weary rebuke of all these goings-on, gave a verdict of accidental death, as though he could not be bothered to fathom why Hapwool should eat the wrong variety. The circumstances of the death surely precluded suicide, for which in any case there was no motive, and suggested so strongly the wayward eccentricities of Oxford dons, that he had no hesitation in ascribing the unfortunate demise of Hapwool simply to some sort of incomprehensible academic playfulness, a kind of wool-gathering brought on by fungus-gathering.

After the inquest we saw Paula Hapwool dressed in her impeccable widow's weeds and ostentatiously narcissistic dark glasses slipping away from the small crowd (which I suppose was actually the largest Caernarfon could muster) and climbing into her Volkswagen in the company of Miller of Merton, whom she appeared to kiss.

'There we are,' I said. 'Doesn't that complete the picture?'

99

For once Speedfall was at a loss. Already deprived of his *idée fixe* about suicide, and now deprived at one stroke of his illusions about both Paula and Miller, he could say nothing. His love of mysteries had not helped him at all, and his impulsive argufying had only led him in circles. As we ourselves finally drove away, rattling dangerously in Speedfall's old car, at last I felt in a position to put him right.

'It's like your principles of classification in a way,' I said. 'You have to modify your view of the truth to accommodate the previously unknown facts. What is the only explanation of Hapwool eating the wrong fungus?'

'You tell me,' said Speedfall, changing up to negotiate a bend.

'There must have been a substitution. By someone who knew what he was doing.'

'Not Paula?'

'I think not. Not expert enough. The whole thing had to be set up and carefully timed as well. I expect she knew about it, though.'

'Miller, then.'

'Of course,' I said. 'That letter was just one of many red herrings, probably deliberately designed to put any investigation off the scent. Miller had to be there at the time, as Hapwool's diary makes clear: the wager was to take place at six o'clock on the fifteenth of July, the day before we arrived, such synchronisation being impossible to supervise at a distance, obviously. Since Hapwool was producing the specimens to be eaten it would be easy for Miller to make the switch, since Hapwool may have believed him to be an idiot but would never have suspected him of being a villain. Miller was in the cottage before we arrived, and knew precisely what would have occurred behind the locked doors.'

'But we overtook him arriving at the cottage,' objected Speedfall.

'No,' I said. 'We thought we did. He had hoped to get away in time, but when he saw our car approaching he simply turned round and walked in the opposite direction, back towards the cottage. That was why Paula Hapwool was so nervous when we arrived. She hadn't expected Miller to be there as well. And she didn't want us to suspect that he'd been there before. Don't you remember her picking up those sunglasses and pretending they were hers?'

'How do you know they weren't?'

'Well, we've just seen her wearing a quite different pair, and those others were far too big for her. They slipped off her nose.'

'Did you realise all this at the time?'

'Not really,' I said. 'Though I thought there was something funny about those hens. You were too busy fooling about with the axe to notice.'

'What about the hens?' said Speedfall. I could see that he was full of admiration for my detective work, since he kept turning to look at me, therefore hitting even more hedges than usual.

'Did you notice that when Miller was talking to you about Hapwool in such scornful terms, one of the things he said was that he couldn't even get the hens to lay?'

'And they weren't laying, as I remember,' said Speedfall.

'Quite,' I said. 'But the Hapwools had only had them for a few days, hadn't they, so how did Miller know?'

'You're right, you're absolutely right. What can we do about it?'

Speedfall looked almost ready to screech to a halt and turn back there and then. He was waiting for an answer, and on this rare occasion I actually believed that he would listen to me.

'Nothing,' I said. 'Nothing at all. We still have a few days left. Let's go and look at some castles.'

The Five Poster Bed

It was, I suppose, a sort of personal challenge, a flyting, a flirtation, a combat of wit, a sexual take-over bid, a hung vote, a philosophical argument, a power struggle, an aunt-complex, a forensic firework display, a piece of secret property-dealing, a love-hate affair. It was almost anything that you could think of, and Speedfall was at the centre of it as usual. With him (or rather against him) was the eighteen-stone American marriagist, Miriam La Fay, possibly the most famous woman of the early eighties and its extraordinary reaction against orthodox feminism.

I don't think that marriagism lasted very long. Not many movements of the kind did. It was like the proliferation of sects in the time of the Civil War: great loyalty was demanded for the obscurest of causes. It was a time when you had to stand up and be counted. Where feminism had rebelled against the orthodox and restrictive role for the woman, marriagism embraced it wholeheartedly. For the marriagist the woman was not only a helpmeet but a willing and swooning slave; she was not only a sex object to be wooed and idolised, she was the pampered shrine of an obsessive tumescent cult; she was not only wife, but perpetual bride.

Where your feminist breathed fire and reason, a sort of

sexual combination of Calvinist tub-thumper and demyth-
ologising theologian, your active marriagist was all blood
and attar-of-roses, the equivalent of heady ritualism and
vatic superstition. Miriam La Fay was best known for her
eight husbands (the least of them a priapic Greek ship-
owner, and most of them dipsomaniac millionaires) and for
her best-selling volume *The Five Poster Bed*, a racy account of
her own enlightened personal career and beliefs.

Speedfall had encountered her on a television book
programme on which he had been induced to appear,
under the impression that it was to debate some recent
trends in academic philosophy. The programme did deal
with philosophy of a kind, mostly Miriam La Fay's. There
was nothing very academic about it. The other participants
were a cross Ulster poet, a boiler-suited actress and a
stuttering defrocked monk. It was a sort of upmarket chat
show, and I could see that Speedfall was angry.

The compère seemed to relish Speedfall's anger. Indeed,
he seemed to think it his job to get all his guests absolutely
seething with hatred. Miriam La Fay insulted the actress for
appearing on political demonstrations, the actress insulted
the monk for weakness of principles, the monk insulted
Speedfall for being unwilling to liberate himself from the
cloister, Speedfall insulted Miriam La Fay for her lack of
a credible philosophy, and the cross Ulster poet insulted
everybody. The compère was extremely happy. Everyone
had, I could see, been plentifully tanked up beforehand,
and there appeared to be several jugfuls of vodkatinis
within range of the camera.

I only watched the programme because Speedfall had
happened to mention it. I hoped that none of the other
Fellows of St Patrick's were watching, because really, it had

to be admitted, Speedfall didn't show himself in a good light at all. The programme was centred on *The Five Poster Bed* on the occasion of its appearance in Britain as a paperback. (Appearance was the right word: it did just suddenly appear, everywhere, in bookshops, railway stations, kiosks – you couldn't buy a razorblade in Boots without it staring up at you from a sort of lobster-pot.) Speedfall kept attacking it on theoretical grounds which seemed in context to have no possible relevance. It was like a Jacques Derrida autopsy on a Mills and Boon. The book itself was, in my opinion, straight gush with the slenderest of abstract arguments, something to do with a defence of the phallocentric society and the ritual subjugation of brides. Speedfall launched into it like a seminar topic, hammering the notion of intention in the early chapter on 'The Efficacy of Wooing.' Miriam La Fay simply ogled him in return, batting eyelashes like bunches of overripe bananas.

It was clear to everyone watching (except Speedfall) that she fancied him like mad. When she announced her plans for an ideal community of real men and women, the qualities needed to survive this latterday voluntary flood sounded very much like the qualities displayed by Speedfall on this occasion: arrogance, aggression, self-confidence, and so on. A certain sort of male rectitude, a kind of smug patriarchal certainty, was also a requisite. And yes, Speedfall was indisputably one of the original Young Fogeys. It made some sort of sense. Though you wouldn't have thought he was bursting with sex appeal in the ordinary sense. His ambience was tweed not denim. His dangerous driving was not masterful but myopic. Perhaps all that sort of thing would make a marriagist swoon. I don't know. He was rather like everyone's memory of their arm-twisting and opinionated elder brother.

Miriam La Fay took the opportunity of plugging this idea she had of a marriagist community. There was, she said, this deserted village by the sea in North Wales, a place of granite and rugged masculine values, a unique site reeking of blood and resistance, a meeting-place of history and human destiny. She had set her heart on it. She meant to buy it, and to found her marriagist community.

There was general scepticism. The actress said it was like burying your head in the sand. The Ulster poet snorted into his vodkatini. The unfrocked monk mildly pointed out that it had taken him ten years of summoned courage to escape from such a place. The compère made some ribald comment to the studio audience, which hooted back with laughter. But Miriam La Fay stood her ground nobly, her comfortable bulk in its pink flounces resilient against such petty and unimaginative barbs. She beamed.

But Speedfall held the trump card.

'Well,' he said. 'There's a simple answer to that. You can't have it.'

'Is that so?' murmured Miriam La Fay seductively. 'Why ever not?'

'Because my College owns it,' said Speedfall triumphantly. 'And we'll never sell it.'

He grinned at the rest of the panel, his collar askew, and adjusted his glasses on his nose as though dotting an i with a flourish.

This didn't put Miriam La Fay off at all. On the contrary, it seemed to increase her interest in Speedfall. She blinked and shrugged excitedly and made a little *moue*. I do believe that if the lights and cameras had not been there she would have gone over and sat on his knee, had it been sturdy enough to bear her weight.

'Is that a challenge, Dr Speedfall?' she twittered. 'Because if it is, I'd like to take you up on it.'

'Not a challenge,' said Speedfall with a foolhardy certainty. 'Simply a fact of life.'

At that point the programme came to an end, lending an odd emphasis to what after all was simply an incidental altercation in the general debate. This meant that it was picked up by several newspaper reviews, and came to the notice of Principal Crocusby in the form of a cutting put on his desk by his ever-vigilant secretary.

'What's this?' said Crocusby. 'Money?'

The Principal was always on the *qui vive* for money. He felt that the College couldn't have enough of it. It was always needed somewhere. Preferably in very large quantities.

'Why did you tell that Valkyrie that she couldn't buy that deserted village in Wales?' he asked Speedfall, when they happened to meet in the Smoking Room. 'It might pay for our new residential block.'

Speedfall simply looked in horror at the Principal and pretended to find something of great interest to read in the *Spectator*. He didn't think the point was to be seriously argued. The land in the parish of Llanbadrig on the Lleyn Peninsula was part of the Founder's original bequest. The foundation stone of the College had been quarried in 1541 from the mountain above the deserted village in question, shipped by sea to Bristol and then brought by a team of horses to Oxford. There was a reference to it in one of the facetious, learned Tudor plays of the time, and the stone itself was visible in the College bar, incised with the initials of generations of St Patrick's undergraduates. The Llanbadrig land was as much a part of the College as its Oxford fabric, unsaleable, inalienable.

Besides, Speedfall wanted nothing more to do with the notorious pink marriagist, however many millions she may have acquired in her long career of acquisitive wedlock. He didn't even want to get married. He didn't want anything to do with any of it.

However, *dis aliter visum* and so forth: he was not to be let off the hook so lightly.

'That terrible woman is after me,' he complained.

'So I understand,' I replied. 'You were seen taking her out to lunch at the Randolph on Tuesday.'

'*She* took *me*,' he objected.

'Well, you surely didn't have to go if you didn't want to.'

'You don't understand,' complained Speedfall. 'She knows Uncle Jeremy. I can't be rude to her.'

'Oh dear, I see.'

'Well, not as rude as I'd like.'

I sympathised. Speedfall was somewhat under his Uncle Jeremy's thumb; Uncle Jeremy was the sort of top civil servant who could say no to a Prime Minister, and as a result no one, least of all an unpractical and financially expectant nephew, could afford to say no to him.

'Are she and your Uncle Jeremy, you know . . . ?'

'Good Lord no,' said Speedfall. 'But she's staying at Tussocks while her divorce comes through.'

'Her divorce?' I exclaimed. 'I didn't know that she was getting divorced again.'

'Oh yes,' said Speedfall. 'She gets them *in absentia* from the States. She probably has some sort of standing order. It must be terribly easy and quick by now, like pregnancy.'

'Who's the lucky number nine?' I asked.

Speedfall looked uneasy, and lowered his voice.

'That's just the trouble,' he said. 'Nobody knows.'

'She seems to have got her eye on you,' I said half-jokingly.

Speedfall cried out in pain.

'Don't!' he exclaimed. 'Don't say things like that. You don't know what you might unwittingly bring about.'

'I didn't know you were superstitious.'

'She is!' answered Speedfall. 'She knew what sign I was born under. She seemed to find it very significant. I had my horoscope in detail during the whole meal. Most embarrassing.'

'And she was paying?'

'It was so difficult,' said Speedfall despairingly. 'She explained that she wanted to make amends. She pretended that she had insulted me on that awful television programme, and wanted to say she was sorry.'

'Whereas,' I put in, 'it was you who had insulted her.'

'Not exactly,' Speedfall objected. 'But anyway, it all seemed so unnecessary. The things she said, too. The whole dining-room could hear.'

I could well imagine it. Someone had once described the erotic quality of Marilyn Monroe's voice as a flute blown through suède: Miriam La Fay's was more like a bassoon blown through marshmallow. She had the sexual magnetism of a blast furnace and was about as embraceable as a small marquee. Speedfall had really not deserved to fall into her clutches.

'And how,' I asked, 'did she propose to make amends, apart from giving you lunch?'

'That's just it,' pondered Speedfall. 'I'm really not at all sure. She gave me a copy of *The Five Poster Bed* specially bound in knicker-coloured silk, but she can't believe that

I'd be delighted. Not after what I'd said about it on the programme.'

'What was she up to, then?' I wondered. 'Perhaps she wanted something from you. Why, after all, should she come and stay with your Uncle Jeremy?'

'Why indeed?' moaned Speedfall. 'It gives her an unwarranted licence to behave like an aunt. I have enough aunts already.'

'She seems a bit too friendly for an aunt to me,' I reflected.

'Oh, you're quite right,' said Speedfall. 'She's much worse than an aunt.'

'She's certainly after something,' I said. 'It's the deserted village.'

'Yes, she asked me all about that again. I told her that the College would never sell. The Bursar wouldn't hear of it for a start. And anyway it's a frightful place, full of weird squatters and tramps. Do you remember those mushroom-worshippers the police threw out just before that Hapwool affair?'

I did remember them, and I remembered the place. It was, in fact, very isolated and very beautiful, a steep valley by the sea cut off from all traffic, heavily wooded and containing roofless granite terraces of quarrymen's cottages. Just the place, I pointed out to Speedfall, for a marriagist commune.

'A commune holds property in common,' he said. 'A marriagist commune seems to me to be a contradiction. Would they all propose to marry each other?'

'I don't think so,' I replied. 'Not simultaneously at any rate.'

'Wouldn't it all be terrifically uncomfortable? She

doesn't seem to be the back-to-nature type.' Speedfall seemed appalled at the conceivable reality of such a commune.

'She's extremely wealthy, isn't she?' I pointed out. 'They'd all have helicopters, and solar heating. And five poster beds.'

'That settles it,' said Speedfall. 'It would be an absolute disaster. I must speak to the Bursar. I must warn him about her.'

These were fine sentiments. Speedfall was in a powerful and resolute mood, and needed no further urging to oppose marriagism. So, even though I'd just remembered a rather suggestive and rhapsodic passage in her book on the subject of plurality of spouses, I kept quiet. He went immediately to warn the Bursar.

Alas, and of course too late. Miriam La Fay had picked up a number of useful tips for her campaign from her lunch with Speedfall, not least the fact of the Bursar's power. She invited him to lunch, too, but this time it was on home ground, and he was to bring another member of the Bursarial Committee, someone 'reliable.'

The attentive reader will have already had ample evidence of my reticence and discretion in these pages. When I reveal that I happened to be a member of the Bursarial Committee at that time it will be readily understood why I am able to give a first-hand account of Miriam La Fay's persuasive powers.

'Good morning, Mrs La Fay. Good morning, gentlemen. Your room is ready. Annabel, the coats! A brisk day for this time of the year, isn't it? I have taken the liberty of putting out a ten-year-old Glenlivet on the side in view of this nasty wind. There is of course the fino, as ordered, very slightly chilled. And your scarf, sir? Thank you. Isabel will take you up.'

It was the proprietress of Porter's herself who welcomed us, daughter or granddaughter (no one quite knew) of the Mrs Porter who had established this celebrated restaurant just before the turn of the century. Behind the green door with the brass knocker in the shape of a garter, generations of Londoners had lunched and dined each other into a state of gustatory bliss and eupeptic cooperation. The Prince of Wales had been an habitué, and it was here that Poire Langtry had been invented (pears stuffed with burned cream and almonds and soused in greengage brandy). T. S. Eliot used to lunch here, since it was situated conveniently near to the London Library. He had written most of his unpublished detective novel at a solitary table in the window. Mrs Porter jealously guarded the manuscript which had been presented to her, and would only show it to her oldest customers. I had been told something about it (the victim is a dried fruit importer who is found drowned in a basement in Lower Thames Street) but would have dearly liked to read it myself. Would I ever be offered a glimpse? It was said to be worth one hundred pounds a page.

Miriam La Fay was divested of her fur coat, revealing her customary pink splendour and a large black handbag like a chained Gutenberg bible.

'After you, my dear Dr Chamfer,' she breathed.

Henry Arthur Chamfer, MA, D.Phil, Estates Bursar and Fellow of St Patrick's, did not believe he was a man easily won. It was, after all, a quality of sheer persistence and integrity (some would say stubbornness) that led him to publish the one piece of academic work that had brought him fame (some would say notoriety), an argument that the sixth century BC Greek poet Alkman was a woman. He later edited and conflated the fragmentary remains of Alkman into a text of more than Sapphic eloquence, but this work, swiftly discredited in the learned journals, was soon remaindered at three-and-sixpence.

Chamfer had been undeterred, and in his capacity as the College Tutor in Classics had accepted for entrance to St Patrick's only those schoolboys who revealed in their papers direct knowledge (and approval) of his theories. The result had been a dramatic decline in the number of his pupils. The day soon arrived when the fact could no longer be concealed that Chamfer had no pupils at all, and there seemed to be no alternative but to make him Estates Bursar, a position which had just then fallen vacant.

It was a tradition in St Patrick's that this position be held in rotation by ordinary Fellows of the College rather than by a professionally competent outsider. Since there were no other demands upon Chamfer's time, and since the rest of us viewed the Bursarship as an onerous duty, the principle of rotation, the last safeguard against incompetence and venality, was quietly abandoned.

The extensive property of St Patrick's was, you might rather dramatically claim, at Chamfer's disposal.

Yet still he did not believe that he was a man easily won. Much water had to flow beneath his bridge before a neighbouring college could acquire a St Patrick's tennis court for use as a car park for their American graduates, for example, and if a voice at a College meeting was raised in mild objection, Chamfer's invariable reply was: 'We have to move with the times, or the times will move us.' If forced on an issue of this sort, he could always pull some sort of rabbit out of his sleeve: a better tennis court in exchange, nearer the College and with electric net-tighteners, or perhaps an offer by the acquisitive college to take all St Patrick's American graduates off their hands.

Revelations of this sort always drew murmurs of quiet confidence. After a while, Chamfer's simple explanation 'We have to move with the times, etc' (which had stood him well in his Alkman days, too) served to placate the College without any further evidence of a profitable bargain, rather as Pavlov's dogs learned to slaver at the mere sound of their dinner bell.

In this way, and without much conscious manipulation on his part, Chamfer acquired power. Rack-renters seeking painless leases on leafy squares in the obscurer parts of north-west London came to eat like doves from his hand. Rustic College tenants stocked his larder with game. Corporation roads were driven across College property with magical ease.

Yet Chamfer thought of himself as astute, a hard bargainer, a principled and inflexible administrator. Indeed he did have principles, and one of them was a love of College history and traditions. About these he knew a great deal, more than the Principal, though not so much perhaps as the History Tutor, Silver Sherwood, who had once undertaken to write a history of the College but had never got round to it. Chamfer relished the age and piety of the foundation, he venerated its buildings and relics, and he cherished its associations. Thus while he might happily relinquish half the College's London property or cover up a tactical error in investment without a qualm of conscience, the thought of proposing to the College that they should lightly part for Mrs La Fay's extraordinary purposes with the birthplace of the Founder, a minor Tudor bishop whom no one (not even Silver Sherwood) remembered for anything but his foundation of the College, was, to put it plainly, unthinkable.

Llanbadrig was remote, the property rugged, the income from it now negligible. And yet the College was named after it and the foundation stone in the beer cellar had come from there. We all toasted the Bishop on Founder's Day, and Silver Sherwood had been to Llanbadrig several times to transcribe the contemporary parish records. To sever such a sacred link would be an idle deed, an act of vandalism. Chamfer had hardly thought twice about it.

But Miriam La Fay had clearly thought a great deal about it. I could see her surveying her quarry with a kind of coquettish cunning. Chamfer's moon face, fringed with tufts of hair of an indeterminate colour, wore a mild and tolerant smile, the smile of an uncle left alone with his niece at an hour too early either for a drink or her bedtime. A pair of substantial executive-type spectacles rested dangerously upon a nose so sharp that it seemed like the point of a compass around which his very circular face had been drawn. He listened to Mrs La Fay's anecdotes about her former husbands, tilting his glass of wheat-coloured scotch, his smile fixed, signalling neither boredom nor encouragement.

'My fourth husband was at Exeter,' she said.

'The college or the university?' asked Chamfer politely.

She was undeterred by this, presumably because the moon face gave no indication as to whether it was a joke or a squelch.

'He was the great explorer,' she replied. 'An Oxford man, of course. He must have been a student in your time.

Sir Toby Forester? He was the first Westerner to penetrate into Tibet, you know.'

'Really?' said Chamfer.

'He did it backwards,' she went on, spitting an olive stone into her chubby fist and conveying it into the fire with the graceful but flirtatious gesture of a Beryl Cook bowls player. 'At each village he was stopped by the secret police and told them he was going to the place he'd just come from.'

'I don't think I remember him,' said Chamfer thoughtfully, as though he were being cross-examined.

I could see that she was going to find it hard work, and I must confess that I sympathised with her. But since she had already written me off as a harmless nonentity, and since Chamfer could bear no brother near the throne, I knew that I could sit back, enjoy my lunch, and be a spectator.

At this moment the waitresses came in, dressed severely like Bill Brandt housemaids. One of them, sloe-eyed and straight-nosed, gave me a very personal smile as she took my empty glass, half-nurse, half-slut. Why couldn't I afford to lunch at Mrs Porter's on my own, I wondered?

The meal began simply, with individual pots of taramasalata at the bottom of which lurked large grey beads of caviare, like turtle eggs buried in sand or a Romanoff necklace unstrung by accident into a cosmetic jar. This was accompanied by dry rye toast, watercress and a few bottles of Louis Roederer of a very safe vintage. Once a few corks had hit the ceiling the party was distinctly merrier.

'One of the reasons why I can believe in husbands,' said Miriam La Fay, 'is that my first one made me extremely rich.'

'Indeed,' said Chamfer.

'His job was to fix the price of gold.'

Chamfer raised his eyebrows.

'I see,' he said, sipping his champagne. The mention of gold was honey to a Bursar's ears.

'Isn't such a thing a fairly automatic procedure?' I asked.

'Oh yes,' said Mrs La Fay. 'But it was great fun. You have to be in touch with the Bank of England, and with various interests in Switzerland. The price moves upwards in units of half a penny until someone wants to sell. So exciting. And you put up the flag if you want to consult your own trading room by telephone. It's like the Boy Scouts.'

She made it seem, indeed, like a harmless hobby. The original Mr La Fay (whose name she had kept, in correct marriagist piety) might just as well in her eyes have been a collector of first-day covers from British Honduras.

'The College still believes in wealth you can stride across,' said Chamfer. 'There's something unreal about gold.'

'Oh, don't say that,' said Mrs La Fay, pained. 'Gold is beautiful.'

She reached forward somewhere in the centre of the table which was dense with cruets, flowers and glass, and pressed a switch. A little shining clockwork train appeared in a circle round the table. Its centre was in fact a wine coaster, holding a bottle of very dry madeira.

Chamfer clapped his hands with delight.

'Oh, how charming!' he exclaimed.

'You couldn't call that unreal, could you?' she asked, stroking the little funnel. 'It's Russian, of course, made for one of the Czars. Mrs Porter only brings such treasures out on very special occasions.'

'But this is just what gold should be used *for*,' said Chamfer with enthusiasm. 'It's very pretty. We could do with one of these in Common Room to ferry the port.'

'Help yourself to the madeira while it's by you, Dr Chamfer,' said Mrs La Fay. 'It goes with the soup.'

At that very moment the waitresses, with their raven bobs and little pearly teeth, entered with the soup, a rich clear amber liquid steaming slightly in fine white porcelain bowls.

'My sixth husband also had a connection with gold,' she went on.

'Was that the art-dealer?' I said, to show her that I was still there and, moreover, that I had done my homework.

'Correct!' she exclaimed, drawing a deep breath and allowing her eyes to travel from my hair to my chin and back again. I froze with my soup spoon in mid-air while she thus assessed me. The moment seemed to last for ever, but eventually she resumed what she was saying and didn't, as I remember, pay me any further attention for the rest of the meal.

'His father was Grossweiler, the German industrialist who in the Twenties managed with great forethought to avoid the simply shocking devaluation of the mark by transferring almost all of his private wealth into gold.'

'Was he allowed to do that?' asked Chamfer.

'There were great difficulties. I won't bore you with details, but he was able to circumvent these difficulties if his gold could be classified as an objet d'art.'

'How was that possible?' inquired Chamfer, adding that it was the best turtle soup that he had ever tasted. 'So glad it is to your tooth, Dr Chamfer,' said Mrs La Fay, 'though to tell no lie it is not turtle but camel, a happy innovation of my fourth husband, the explorer. The greenish fatty diced substance which led you to believe that it was turtle is cut from the hump.'

Chamfer gave a little bow.

'To continue,' said Mrs La Fay. 'Grossweiler took all his gold (ingots, Austrian ducats, US twenty dollar double eagles, kilo bars, everything) to be melted down and cast into a piece of sculpture. He wanted the shape to be as convenient as possible, nothing baroque. He knew little about art, so consulted his son, my future husband, who was something of a disappointment to him, a Bohemian and, as he thought, a wastrel.'

(Camel? I wondered.)

'My husband borrowed a suitable egg-like piece from an artist friend, who was tickled pink by the idea of having it cast in gold. All well so far, but the long and short of it was that when Grossweiler came to want to sell some of the gold, long after the time of the financial crisis, lo and behold if his artistic lump wasn't worth a few millions more, and about the only gold sculpture since Benvenuto Cellini. He'd actually lose a lot of money if it was melted down, but it wasn't much use to him as it was. He hated the sight of it.'

'There's a moral in that somewhere,' said Chamfer.

I privately reflected that the moral was probably that if you want to end up as a wealthy woman you must choose your husbands with care. The golden Arp was probably sitting on her coffee table at that moment.

The next course was a surprise. There was a little flutter of preparation from the waitresses, the lights went out, and Mrs La Fay leaned over winningly and whispered: 'A small token of my esteem' in Chamfer's ear.

A flickering glow appeared out of the darkness, followed by Mrs Porter, who was bearing it like a new-born infant.

It was a small cake with a candle.

'Happy birthday, Dr Chamfer,' said Mrs La Fay.

Chamfer was astounded.

'How on earth did you know it was my birthday?' he demanded. 'I had forgotten myself. I don't believe that I've celebrated my birthday these twenty years.'

'Birthdays are important, Dr Chamfer,' said Mrs La Fay. 'A woman remembers. A mother remembers. A marriagist mother in particular remembers. Birth is the sacramental gratitude of the bride for the favours of her husband.'

Chamfer wiped away a tear and blew out the candle.

'They couldn't get sixty-five candles on,' said Mrs La Fay.

'It doesn't matter,' said Chamfer, in a voice thick with emotion. 'Shall I cut it?'

'Aha,' said Mrs Porter, who had been standing to one side, her arms folded beneath her Edwardian bosom. 'Second surprise!'

She lifted up the supposed cake, a mere shell of cardboard and icing, and revealed a hot mass of something beneath it.

Chamfer put down his knife in amazement. An unusually pungent aroma rose from the plate, sweet and meaty (or was it fishy?). It *looked* like meat, though its shape was strange, somewhat cylindrical, if imperfectly so. The waitresses hovered with decanters like a pair of blackbirds.

'Let me explain, Dr Chamfer,' said Mrs La Fay. 'I thought it would be rather, shall we say, distinctive to celebrate your birthday by having one course in which we would eat only food which was also celebrating its birthday, *your* date of birth, and was therefore as old as you are.'

'Words fail me,' gasped Chamfer.

'What you see before you is a dish created by the famous Escoffier, of whom you have no doubt heard?'

I thought for a moment that she was going to claim Escoffier as one of her husbands.

'I do believe that the College chef is supposed to follow his methods,' said Chamfer, as some of the dish was spooned carefully on to our plates.

'Escoffier has been long dead, of course,' said Mrs La Fay, 'but this boeuf en daube was created by his hand. Do taste the wine, by the way. It is Château Mouton Rothschild 1917. It took a little time to find.'

Dazed, Chamfer sipped. I lifted my own glass.

It was like nothing I had ever tasted before.

'All right?' asked Mrs La Fay, anxiously.

'All right indeed,' gulped Chamfer.

'Apparently Escoffier was asked to supervise the provision of rations for the higher echelons of the French army during the First World War. Occasionally, but very occasionally, quite senior officers were compelled to visit the front line, and even to eat there. Some very acceptable food was put in cans for this purpose. Where did we track this down, Mrs Porter?'

'In the Imperial War Museum, madam,' said Mrs Porter.

'Of course,' said Mrs La Fay. 'A little help from Sir Jeremy there. It was fun getting the year right. The codes on the tin, you know.'

We ate in respectful silence.

One could say that Chamfer was won over at that point, inasmuch as he was ever totally won over. He relaxed and beamed. His sharp nose twinkled.

'I can't say that I properly understand what you want the Llanbadrig land *for*, Mrs La Fay,' he said. 'Is it indeed wholly proper?'

'Wholly proper and serious, Dr Chamfer,' she replied. 'The price offered shows that.'

'Yes, indeed,' agreed Chamfer. The price was ridiculous, and its full extent had not until now been made apparent. It bore about the same relation to its market value as the lunch we were still enjoying bore to the normal business meal being eaten at that moment all over London. The claret itself couldn't have cost less than two hundred pounds a bottle.

'The marriagist movement has very widespread support, and of course my personal wealth is entirely at the movement's disposal.'

'Of course,' said Chamfer.

'And there is always enough to go round,' added Mrs La Fay meaningfully, setting the train in motion so that the hock stood invitingly at Chamfer's hand.

After such a symbolic, and one might say eccentric, entree, Miriam La Fay had arranged a sober pudding, one designed rather to appeal to the heart than the stomach (or the pocket) though it was one that did not fail to delight Chamfer.

'St Patrick's Mulberry Pie!' he cried, after the first mouthful. 'I haven't had it since I was a very junior Fellow, before our old chef died. The recipe was supposed to have been lost in the war. How did you discover it?'

'My dear Dr Chamfer,' cooed Mrs La Fay. 'I have to

confess to you that it was already known to Mrs Porter. Though I hasten to add that she has never served it to anyone before, and has promised never to serve it to anyone in the future.'

The risk paid off. Chamfer was touched by the confession, almost as touched as he was to be eating St Patrick's Mulberry Pie.

Miriam La Fay timed her next remark perfectly.

'She says that she will let you have the recipe to take back to Oxford. It might be rather a *coup* for you to serve it at the next Founder's Day.'

I could see that Chamfer was making a resolution that he would serve it first at a dinner of his own, to which he would invite and infinitely surprise Silver Sherwood.

The thought of taking Silver Sherwood down a peg or two would amuse him greatly.

The lunch still had a few delectable courses in hand, but the essential work was done. Indeed, I don't think I had ever seen it done better. The sale was barely mentioned, but Mrs La Fay knew, and Chamfer knew that Mrs La Fay knew, and Mrs La Fay knew that Chamfer knew that Mrs La Fay knew that he would now be quietly and persistently on the side of marriagism and primitive wedlock rituals in North Wales.

The *coup de grâce* was delivered in the lobby as Isabel and Annabel eased us into the embrace of our overcoats, snugger than when we had entered. There was a long large box on the table.

'Oh, by the way, Dr Chamfer,' said Mrs La Fay. 'That's for you.'

'For me, Miriam?' exclaimed Chamfer.

'Absolutely . . . Henry,' said Mrs La Fay.

Inside the box, wrapped in white tissue and complete with all its accessories, was the little golden train.

Still swimming with the food and wine, Chamfer was finally speechless. I had to take his arm.

'Just think,' said the enormous priestess of marriagism. 'You can have a real wing-ding at your college.'

It is a good example of Speedfall's wonderfully vulnerable and innocent sort of self-obsessed obtuseness, that despite having all this bribery related to him at the earliest opportunity he continued to believe that Miriam La Fay regarded him (and not Chamfer) as the key to her hopes. I had seen something of his odd view of women before in the case of the girl in the cheese shop (a story that had better remain untold) and to a certain extent in the business with Paula Hapwool. Put it down to his inexperience. Any relationship with a woman, fraught as it was with a possibly wholly theoretical but nonetheless certainly theoretically possible sexual interest, became a minefield of misunderstandings.

'She's after me again,' he would say, having glimpsed her across the room at a publisher's launch. I suppose in fairness to Speedfall you do more than 'glimpse' eighteen stone: it must have seemed as pointed a sighting as a Descent of Juno, or the Wife of Bath at a convention of Pardoners. I think he was beginning to feel the effect of her interest in him, but persisted in ascribing it to her desire for the College's land rather than her desire for his angular body. Perhaps he was so used to the onerous business of pleasing aunts that any female presence with the hint of a challenge brought out the short-trousered nephew that he had once been.

Somewhere inside him this prep-school ghost was saying: 'No, I won't go to tea! I don't *want* a five pound postal order!' But much deeper down, or so I reckoned, the siren call of the marshmallow bassoon lured from him a more fundamental response: 'Give! Give me your essence! Give me the marrow of your being!' the voice murmured to him, and his It, longing to be a husband, had begun to scratch its way out of the cloister of his philosophising mind like the Count of Monte Cristo. The only thing was, it would take him a lifetime to escape.

Meanwhile, Miriam La Fay remained worse than an aunt. And, because she was not really an aunt, actually resistible. He would oppose the sale of the Llanbadrig land with every ounce of cunning he could summon. If the Bursar had weakened, that only strengthened his own resolve.

For myself, I was upset about the proposed sale not so much for reasons of historical sentiment, and not particularly through a dislike of marriagism, but simply because the College's cottages there were often let to Fellows. It was a familiar haven, a retreat from the pressures of library and laboratory. I didn't see why we should give that up, as no doubt we would have to, under the pressure of unwarranted financial gain.

Payne, who had one of the cottages, and went there frequently, was visibly outraged.

'It's absolutely typical of Chamfer,' he said, waving the agenda of the next College meeting in my face as I poured myself coffee one evening in the Smoking Room. 'Slip it in anywhere, between a vacant Chair and the date of the next Gaudy, hope no one will notice and all say Yes like good little boys.'

Speedfall, who had overheard him, smiled seraphically.

'Patience,' he said. 'He'll need a two-thirds majority, because it would need a repeal of statute, of course.'

'Of course,' echoed Payne, to whom this was as much news as it was to me.

'It's only my opinion, naturally,' said Speedfall, 'but the statute can certainly be taken that way.'

When Speedfall had gone (to give a talk to an undergraduate society, the title being, so he claimed, 'Who was to blame: Voltaire or Rousseau?') Payne and I turned with one mind to look in the bookcase for the College *Statutes*. Was there really a statute forbidding the sale of this particular College property? I couldn't remember it, but the possibility was distinctly encouraging.

Poor Payne: he rented his own cottage in Llanbadrig direct from the Bursary for a token sum and had often approached Chamfer about the possibility of purchasing it outright. Chamfer had always stalled, with eloquent explanations about the historical importance of the Founder's bequest. Now it was proposed to sell off the lot to some dubious free-love cult! But I was bound to point out to him that Miriam La Fay's kind of love was not free but sacramentally secure, not free but expensive, not free but engaged. He grunted at that.

'It sounds suspiciously polygamous to me,' he said. 'A sort of female Mormonism.'

Together we flipped through the yellowing pages of the *Statutes* until we came to what surely had to be the relevant passage, since strangely enough it contained the only reference to Llanbadrig in the entire volume:

'5. *All the rents, quit rents, rack rents and all income whatsoever (including such sums as shall from time to time be determined as*

*accruing, after due deductions for administrative expenses, from sale
of timber, fishing rights and agricultural stock owned by the College)
from the land west of the Afon Siaradus in the parish of Llanbadrig,
shall be applied solely for the purpose of providing a College Feast or
Entertainment in celebration of the Founder and for no other purpose
save, at the discretion of the Principal and Fellows, in the event of a
substantial deficit in the Endowment Account.'*

'Good old Speedfall,' said Payne. 'I must have a chat
with him about the legal implications of this excellent
Statute Five.'

I couldn't but agree, although I was aware that Speedfall
was a philosopher not a lawyer, and that the Law in all its
manifestations (including College Statutes) maintained a
shifting, evasive, relative, linguistic, even poetic, relationship with the Absolute Truth.

The Absolute Truth in Payne's opinion was that Chamfer
was an absolute stinker, and during the next few days he
made little secret of this view. The unfortunate result of this
was that the more conservative members of the Governing
Body rallied to the support of the Bursar, who was, after all,
a responsible senior Fellow and a College Officer with a
difficult and unrewarding job to do. Was young Payne
suggesting that there was some kind of disloyalty in this
proposal of Chamfer's? Surely he must realise that the
Bursar had a deep love of the College? Why, only last week
he had presented to the Senior Common Room a most
expensive Russian toy designed to relieve members of
fatiguing decanter-humping. This was not the gesture of a
disloyal Fellow. But was it not true that Payne himself had
a personal interest in this obscure Welsh property? Now
that seemed a rather significant element in the affair . . .

Needless to say, however, Payne found much support

among the less blinkered members of the College. Grolier, the economist, wondered what the College would do with the income from the sale and observed dourly that it was a risky moment to invest on the Stock Market. The Dean felt that the whole proposal diminished the charisma of the founding Bishop and therefore constituted an obscure attack upon organised religion in the College. The English Fellow, Ted Wigan, in one of his Maoist moods, said he was opposed to all proposals affecting the College's extensive wealth from a conviction that they were made only in order to increase it. Silver Sherwood was simply opposed to Chamfer on personal grounds, and Speedfall, of course, was opposed to Miriam La Fay. A curious assortment of allies, but on the basis of a necessary two-thirds majority for the proposal, it had the makings of a serious opposition.

Speedfall was convinced that if we sold her the land, the College would never get rid of her.

'She would found a Chair of Marriagism,' he complained. 'She would pile bequest upon bequest. The College would be so much in her debt that it would have to be renamed La Fay College, and we would have baseball and cheerleaders and sophomores. And the Bursar would become husband no. 9.'

Crocusby was certainly aware that we were all concerned about the La Fay offer. His various spies told him that something was in the air. The Bursarial Committee should have considered it first, naturally, but it was not for me to complain. Crocusby didn't particularly care for the idea of selling the Llanbadrig property, but he had learned to trust Chamfer and there was now a well-established tradition which said that he should support him, too. There was some sense in this. If the College lost confidence in Chamfer they would need a new Bursar, and it would be the Principal's difficult task to find one. Not that they were anywhere near getting into that particular boat, for which, no doubt, Crocusby was more than grateful.

There was another reason why he should give his approval to the proposal. A number of the senior Fellows had indicated to him that the College would be well pleased, when they extended the Back Quad to the south to form a new residential block overlooking the Warden of Wadham's garden, that the block should be given his name in token of his devotion to the College and of his long reign as Principal. The College didn't have an unlimited income, and many of those who had a hand in this rash and syco-phantic gesture had felt that it might never be realised, not in their (or Crocusby's) lifetimes at any rate. Crocusby was not prepared to accept the new block as a mere Quixotic tribute, a College pipe-dream to impress Important Old Members, or indeed as anything but a solid plan to be put into immediate operation as soon as they had a spare half a million or so.

And might there not be half a million forthcoming from Miriam La Fay?

The more he thought about this, the more he was determined to have no nonsense from the meeting, no hair-splitting from Speedfall, no sentimental gush from Silver Sherwood. I could see as he came into the meeting that he was going to support Chamfer to the hilt. As he sat down in his chair his eyes glittered accusingly from beneath his wiry eyebrows, and the hair that curled from his nostrils twitched slightly. He was like some caged animal whom it would be dangerous to provoke.

Chamfer looked confident.

Some routine business was dispatched, and we came to the item laconically described in the agenda as 'Llanbadrig.'

'A paper has been circulated, I believe,' said the Principal, as though the fact amounted to an unwarranted concession which had put an unwelcome burden on the College Secretary.

'Yes, and I think it's disgraceful,' said Silver Sherwood.

'Perhaps,' said the Principal icily, 'the Bursar would like first to speak to the proposal.'

Chamfer rose, and his round face beamed blandly round the room.

'We all have to move with the times,' he began, launching into his exposition. He said nothing that the meeting did not already know. Indeed, he virtually said nothing, but he said it with great charm and eloquence.

Professor Tort, holder of the Judge Jeffreys Chair of Jurisprudence, was as usual much impressed. Absolved by the nature of his academic position from any obligation to be concerned with College administration, he nonetheless staunchly supported the College establishment.

'. . . clear-headed about this . . .' Chamfer was saying.

Professor Nought, octogenarian incumbent of the University's Chair of Negative Mathematics, thought of himself as being exceptionally clear-headed. It looked as though Chamfer was, too, so he might as well support the man. Professor Nought should have retired almost two decades ago, but no one was quite sure how old he was and now the chance had been missed.

'. . . make no bones about it . . .' said Chamfer.

Professor Wart, head of the Physiology Department, woke up at the word 'bones', saw that Chamfer was making some sort of motion, resolved to vote in favour of it, and then went back to sleep.

'. . . enlightened experiment in community life . . .' murmured Chamfer.

Professor Ought, who held the Immanuel Kant Chair of Compulsive Philosophy, ground his teeth together at the sight of Speedfall, who sat at the other end of the table, smug and ready, with his finger in a well-used copy of the *Statutes*. He had heard that Speedfall would have a number of obstructive points to make, and resolved to have nothing to do with the philosophical upstart. He would vote for Chamfer all along the line.

'. . . and so, gentlemen,' concluded Chamfer, 'I believe that we should take advantage of this extremely generous offer.'

He sat down.

'Hear, hear,' said the Dean. 'It seems a very realistic proposal.'

'It's a shocking proposal, if I may say so, Principal,' said Silver Sherwood, 'and I am surprised that the Bursar should be making it. He must be aware, as are we all, of the traditions linking this College with the village of Llanbadrig, traditions which are to say the very least of it inalienable.'

'May I answer that, Principal?'

Crocusby graciously inclined his head.

'These traditions,' said Chamfer, 'will not cease to exist. They are part of our history. As everyone knows, I am myself very proud of this College's history. I don't think that any of us has a monopoly of feelings of that sort.'

'Hear, hear,' interrupted the Dean, for the second time.

'But we can't live in the past. This College needs to

expand, to meet the needs of the undergraduate of today, and to cater for the needs of the undergraduate of tomorrow. This seems to me, and I believe I speak for the Principal too, a most timely and generous offer.'

'At this moment, Principal,' said Grolier, 'the College would be well advised to retain its agricultural property. When we move out of the Common Market . . .'

'Yes, well, I dare say,' said Crocusby, interrupting hastily. 'There are lots of different views on this point. You may be right, who knows?' He laughed shortly, as if to imply that Grolier could not, under any circumstances, ever be right.

After a few more exchanges of this sort, Speedfall made his barbed intervention. I looked at him as he delivered his first salvo and felt that I could almost see, hovering about his head, the armoured object of his hostility and gathered resources, the challenging Valkyrie of committed matrimony. He was pale, icy, tense, a man with every appearance of being on active service.

'We do realise,' he said, 'that before we can pass this motion, before we can put it, even, we should have to repeal Statute Five?'

There was much rustling of papers and leafing through pages. 'We've all read Statute Five, I suppose?' said Crocusby, with infinite weariness.

A mutter of unconvincing assent went round the room.

'Shall I read it?' asked Speedfall. He proceeded to read it without waiting for an answer.

Ted Wigan, who was sitting next to me, whispered: 'And how much *do* we spend on this historic annual feast, I would like to know?'

I shrugged. I hoped that Wigan would not make such a point publicly, because it would lose a lot of support that might otherwise now materialise. There were not many Fellows who did not deeply relish Founder's Day.

'You see my point?' said Speedfall. 'We shall have to repeal this statute, and that means taking it to the Privy Council.'

'And to the University,' said Silver Sherwood.

'We've done that before,' said Crocusby. 'There's no problem about repealing a statute.'

'I was just pointing it out,' said Speedfall. 'And naturally to repeal it we should need a two-thirds majority.'

There was a short pause.

'I wonder if that is right, Principal?' asked Professor Ought, with ill-concealed glee. 'Has Dr Speedfall read this statute? I know he has read it to us. And he read it quite well, I thought. But has he read it to himself?'

There was laughter.

'The point seems to me, Principal,' continued Professor Ought, leaning back in his chair, 'to be what we do or do not do with the Llanbadrig income. If we were proposing to spend it on psychical research, or wallpaper, or planting an orchard in the front quadrangle, then I agree: we would need to repeal the statute. The statute expressly says that we must spend this income on Founder's Day celebrations and on nothing else.'

He smiled round the room, letting his glance fall in polite malice on Speedfall.

'But, gentlemen,' Professor Ought went on, 'this is not what we are doing. We are intending to abandon all rights to the income from this Welsh parish. This income will pass to Mrs La Fay, a person not bounden, I believe, by the

Statutes of the College? Thus we may in theory still abide by the Statute. All our income from this source *will* continue to be applied to the stated annual celebration. There will simply have ceased to be any income.'

'I am very grateful to Professor Ought for his learned judgment,' said Chamfer, with a small bow.

'With all due respect to Professor Ought,' said Speedfall, unabashed, 'this isn't quite the case, I think.'

Chamfer froze.

'You see,' said Speedfall, 'if the Statute referred to all the rents etcetera etcetera from the land etcetera etcetera *owned by the College*, then Professor Ought would be right. Once we ceased to own the land the Statute would no longer apply, though it might, I venture to suggest, be applicable to the proceeds of the sale.'

'You bet,' said Ted Wigan.

Professor Ought assumed an expression of mock-incredulity.

'Dr Speedfall surprises me,' he said. 'I asked a minute ago if he had read the Statute. Now I am tempted to ask if he can read.'

I became uneasy. Payne was looking miserable. Ted Wigan was doodling a firing-squad on his blotter, altering the recognisable features of the victim with each stage of the argument. The meeting was certainly getting bogged down in detail. I supposed it was all ultimately necessary.

'The phrase is there,' said Professor Ought, 'the very phrase that Dr Speedfall postulated!' He quoted: 'All the rents etcetera including such sums etcetera from the sale of this that and the other *owned by the College*.'

He sat back triumphantly.

'With all due respect,' said Speedfall, 'it is there, but it is in the wrong place.'

All eyes were bent to their copies of the statute.

'It applies only to the matter within the parentheses. I don't see how it could possibly apply to the main sentence outside those parentheses. It's a simple matter of English prose.'

Speedfall looked across at Ted Wigan. Wigan, who was sketching an extensive pool of blood beneath the crumpling feet of Professor Ought, caught the glance and said hastily:

'I agree, of course.'

Principal Crocusby looked sour, and Professor Ought abandoned all further interest in the meeting.

Chamfer looked round urbanely.

'Let us not take all this too ponderously,' he said sweetly. 'I'm sure we shall be safe in assuming that Statute Five must be repealed.'

At this point Silver Sherwood said his piece, favouring the meeting with a detailed history of the origins of the College. It was a tedious ramble, a monstrous balloon of a speech, quietly deflated by Chamfer who pointed out that the past was the past, immutable and inviolable, that the Llanbadrig parish records and other documents would remain intact, that the obscure Tudor bishop's bones could still be visited. In short, everything would remain more or less the same.

'Our friend Payne has an interest in that area as some of you know,' was Chamfer's last stroke, 'and we shall naturally do everything we can to safeguard it.'

He smiled at the scowling Payne.

'The Bishop's bones,' muttered Silver Sherwood savagely.

Professor Wart, who was sitting next to him, woke up at the word 'bones', just in time to vote.

Crocusby seized the opportunity.

'Can we have a show of hands, then, gentlemen?' he asked.

Prettihow, Secretary to the Governing Body and Tutor in Chemistry, rose to count the votes.

'Those in favour?' said the Principal.

A rash of hands shot up. I looked round.

Curidge. The Dean. Campling (of course as Senior Tutor he would support Chamfer). Professors Tort, Nought, Wort and Ought (a particularly vehement fist, this last one). Chamfer, of course. Two of the Junior Research Fellows (what *were* their names?). Lindsay, the Vice-Principal. Prettihow himself. And then the Principal, with both hands up (the Principal having two votes).

'. . . twelve, thirteen, fourteen,' said Prettihow, noting the figure.

'You counted me twice, I hope,' said Crocusby comfortably. Prettihow indicated that he had.

'Now,' said Crocusby threateningly. 'Those against!'

A sprinkling of hands.

My own, of course. Payne's, who put it up as high as it could go, like a schoolboy wanting to be excused. Wigan's hand was up. Mutch, the deaf organist. Silver Sherwood. Grolier. Speedfall. And – wait! – someone else. The third Junior Research Fellow, who forgot to vote the first time and thought that he might as well vote now as not at all.

'Eight,' said Prettihow.

'Well now,' breathed Crocusby. 'Fourteen out of twenty-one present. That's the two-thirds majority, I believe.'

It had to be admitted. It was.

Chamfer was sorting his papers in preparation for the next item on the agenda, and sorting them with evident satisfaction, when Speedfall coughed meaningfully and offered the following observation:

'I hate to say this, but I rather think that in cases where we are voting to repeal a statute we should not count the Principal's two votes.'

'What's that?' said Crocusby, who had been thinking fondly of the new block and was now beginning to feel that if Speedfall was allowed to go on much longer he would be fated not to see it in his own lifetime. 'I can vote twice. I always do. It's in the *Statutes*, unless you all want to repeal that one instead.'

'I didn't say that you couldn't vote twice, Principal,' said Speedfall patiently. 'Simply that you couldn't be counted twice.'

Professor Ought here groaned audibly, and there was much shifting about in seats, lighting of pipes and murmurs of scandal and delight.

It all turned, Speedfall firmly pointed out, on a difference of phrasing between the College statute on voting at College meetings and the relevant clause in the Oxford and Cambridge Act of 1923 governing the procedure for repeal of College Statutes. The first spoke of a 'majority of votes of those present and voting,' the second (in unfortunate conflict with the first, Speedfall agreed) only on a 'two-thirds majority of those present and voting.'

'If, therefore, we count *those voting* in favour of the recent motion,' said Speedfall, 'rather than the *votes cast* for that motion, we come to the inescapable conclusion that, since thirteen is not two-thirds of twenty-one, the motion has not been carried.'

'And therefore we can't proceed to the sale,' added Silver Sherwood delightedly. 'A Daniel come to judgment!'

Though the point could hardly have been made more clearly, it was run through a number of times by different members of the Governing Body for each other's benefit.

'Could it not be maintained,' offered Curidge, with some obtuseness, 'that for this purpose the Principal is two persons?'

'One might think,' supported Chamfer, 'that was the essential idea in the first place. It's nothing to do with the Principal's casting vote, which he may employ in the case of a deadlock.'

'Do you mean to say,' asked Ted Wigan with infinite scorn, 'that there are occasions when the Principal can vote *three* times?'

'I'm afraid so,' I whispered. 'Be quiet.'

'How can the Principal be two persons?' asked Silver Sherwood. 'It's absurd.'

The Dean maintained that as far as he could see the *Statutes* and the Act meant, or were intended to mean, more or less the same thing and that they were all quibbling about nothing.

'Not at all,' said Speedfall eagerly, and I could see that curiously hectic and intense light come into his eyes that always appears when he embarks with constructive confidence upon a philosophical argument. 'It makes a great deal of difference in fact, and it's impossible to judge intention in this matter without being able to ask questions of those who drafted the relevant documents. If, to take an analogy, I were to propose to confiscate all the Fellows' neckties, this would presumably yield a different result than if I proposed to confiscate all the neckties of all the

Fellows, because in the latter case I would discover that the Principal was wearing two neckties. Or had a second neck-tie in his pocket.'

'I'm not wearing a necktie,' said Wigan.

'That,' said Speedfall, 'would be the equivalent of abstaining.'

A few days later I was reflecting on these events in the Front Quad with Speedfall.

'You did well,' I said. 'Now that it's been passed to the Statutes Committee nothing will be done during this academic year at least.'

'It only needed time,' agreed Speedfall. 'We'll make the right decision in the end.'

'Chamfer is upset,' I said.

'Serves him right,' replied Speedfall.

It was a rather fine autumn day, the leaves already turned and spinning now and then to the lawn. Speedfall had just collected some examination papers from the Lodge, and they too were spilling about his feet as though he were deciduous.

'There are things that are far more important, anyway,' he said, dropping a few more.

'Do you think that Miriam La Fay will leave you alone now?' I asked.

'Of course,' he said. 'If we'd sold her the land she'd have been all over me – and the College. I think I did the College some service. Let her found a La Fay College in Illinois' (he pronounced the s) 'we want nothing of it.'

'What do you think she is really up to now?' I won-dered.

'I should think that at this very moment she is ordering

bridal cake and floral displays for marriage number nine, and good luck to her.'

Speedfall was wrong. At that very moment Miriam La Fay was hastening from the College car park through to the Front Quad, in company with his Uncle Jeremy. I nodded towards them with a wry smile, and he turned round in horror.

'Dear boy!' exclaimed Sir Jeremy Speedfall. 'Forgive us for descending on you, but when Miriam heard the news she insisted that I drive her up.'

Miriam La Fay advanced upon Speedfall, who now stood rooted amongst his fallen papers like a recusant martyr heaped with faggots. Her arms were raised. She was wearing something red.

I had visions of violence. The whole scene was strikingly plotted, like a happening. Here then, was Speedfall's come-uppance. But I was wrong: the arms descended not in blows but an embrace.

'At last!' she cried. 'I've found a real man at last!'

She held him at rapturous arms' length, like the recognition scene in Elizabethan comedy. Speedfall was unable to protest.

'Milk-sops,' she said. 'Lily-livered milk-sops, all of them. Lying with their bellies uppermost, waiting to be tickled. Yielding. What woman with red blood in her veins wants a man who yields? I want a man who resists. I want a man who knows his own mind.'

'But, but . . .' objected Speedfall.

Sir Jeremy looked on fondly, like Pandarus.

'Most men would have yielded,' she continued. 'I hoped you wouldn't. You didn't! You held out against me to the end. It was you! It was all your doing that the vote went against me. You marvellous . . . brute!'

Let's leave this happy scene. I don't say that the mis-judgment was a serious one. Sir Jeremy, I think, should take most of the blame. At the time I was too amused to be very much concerned. I knew that that magnificent brute Speedfall would live to tell the tale.

The Smallest Ghost
in the World

———

The College seems to close in upon itself in November. The days are short and the air is crisp, and it always seems to be a crepuscular five o'clock, with people hurrying everywhere, anxious to be indoors: muddied games players clattering past the Lodge with plumes of breath like carthorses; visitors for tea; the chattering crocodile of choristers arriving for evensong; kitchen boys bringing in trays; the occasional undergraduate running unwillingly to a tutorial; a muffled solitary returning from a river walk still with an aura of mist about him but already thinking of the open book beside the fireplace, the new tape of *Tosca* and the packet of chocolate digestive biscuits. Such a scene could hardly have changed much for five hundred years. The College is a place of simple traditions, simple pleasures, hopes and regrets, all centred upon an essentially lonely pursuit of an idea. Sometimes the idea is glimpsed and the chase becomes excited: a footprint here and there, a branch left swinging, a scrap of evidence, a scent upon the air. For most of the time, however, there is merely observation of the procedures, the ordered sharing of hints and clues, those necessary foundations of an institution of religion and learning. But what of the idea itself? What was the nature of its truth? In what form might it ever reveal itself? Would we recognise it if it did?

I was talking about this one night with Speedfall, thinking that a philosopher might have something useful to say about the subject. I was at pains to make it clear that I was indeed talking about a philosophical truth and not a spiritual one. I suppose I was postulating the consummation of the disciplines, not an access of revelation. I'm not superstitious.

But Speedfall had been behaving strangely all through dinner.

'Not superstitious?' he echoed. 'Why not? Why not be superstitious?'

He spoke so loudly, and with such agitation, that Curidge's guest, an already thoroughly intimidated young research fellow from a college in the Banbury Road, jumped and sent a small maelstrom of claret into the air. Several heads turned.

'I don't hink you've really been listening to what I've been saying,' I complained.

'I'm sorry,' said Speedfall, abstractedly. 'I have really, you know, but look at this.'

He was shaking the salt cellar at the edge of his plate, but nothing was coming out.

'Try another one. It's the damp, you know.'

'It's not the damp at all,' shouted Speedfall. 'The thing's perfectly all right.'

More heads turned, and the Principal raised his enormous eyebrows. The under-Butler came round to Speedfall's chair, and asked if anything was the matter.

'No, no. Nothing,' muttered Speedfall.

At that moment the salt came out of the salt cellar. It

came out in an abundant dry stream of white crystals, steady as an hourglass, forming dunes all over Speedfall's plate and over the table.

'You see?' he exclaimed triumphantly, looking around.

'Not really,' I said. 'But never mind.'

Speedfall's behaviour at High Table became stranger and stranger. On one occasion he touched the stem of his wine glass and sent it spinning. On another, he slapped the table in several places with an accelerated rapidity. When finally he stood on his chair during dessert, stamping slightly with his foot, things had clearly got somewhat out of hand. Hall became quite popular, with undergraduates flocking in to see what he would do next. There was a small black market in meal tickets. The Principal had him over into the Lodgings for a serious talk, but according to the Dean could get nothing coherent out of him.

I felt a concern for poor Speedfall. Whatever the doubtful state of his social skills, he had a clear and logical mind and was, by all accounts, good at his subject. It was frightful to think of the ruin of an academic career so early in life. I have had reason to recount elsewhere the many occasions on which his energetic impetuosity or misjudgment had brought him to a pretty pass. He was a genius at mild chaos, an impresario of obtuseness – but I had never thought him mad. Ted Wigan was convinced that it was the natural consequence of a concentration on the episte-mological. 'It must be the fate of all Oxford philosophers to go mad,' he remarked placidly, 'since their subject is in any case so totally out of touch with any form of social reality.' I didn't agree with this, naturally, and not only because I suppose that Speedfall is actually a friend of mine and needed some real sympathy, but because I felt that something in particular was wrong, and I didn't think it had much to do with his mind.

The thing came to a head one Thursday night. Fellows had not been anxious to seat their guests next to Speedfall, and there had initially been much quiet manoeuvring and jockeying for position, so that he had found himself right at the end of the table, next to the most junior fellows, temporary lecturers with dining rights, assistant chaplains, and so on. They were as nervous as anyone about what Speedfall might do, but were less likely to complain. They ate quickly, too shy even to talk to each other, let alone to Speedfall who had, in any case, rather given up conversation at dinner. The meal was pretty much without incident until the pudding arrived. When it was handed to Speedfall, he reached out and instead of taking his helping he pressed down on the dish with his hand, causing poor old Jenkins, who was serving, to have to use all his strength to keep the thing from crashing to the floor. A wild look had come into Speedfall's eyes, and he half rose from his chair. If the pudding had been an innocent and commonplace apricot soufflé (say) the element of humour in the encounter might have won the day. But this guest night was the one chosen by Chamfer to put on display the long-lost St Patrick's Mulberry Pie, the fruit of his weakening to the charms of Miriam La Fay. There had already been much excited curiosity over the appearance of this pudding. Its entry into the Hall had, indeed, been greeted by a sprinkling of applause (some of it, to be fair, ironic).

Now Speedfall and Jenkins confronted each other over the Mulberry Pie with the contained energy of arm wrestlers, and it would have been hard to say which looked the more surprised. Those fellows who had already been served paused in fascinated horror with their spoons in mid-air. Those who had not yet been served were equally horrified, but were also anxious for the fate of their pudding. Some undergraduates in the body of the hall stood up to get a better view, and one of them ventured to wave a football rattle which he had smuggled into dinner in the hope of just such an event.

The outcome was predictable. In his time Jenkins had been a masterful batsman, and even now could reach the boundary in the annual College servant's match against St Patrick's, Cambridge. His hands were sinewy with grubbing up frosty artichokes on his allotment. He was certainly not going to drop the pudding if he could help it. Speedfall, who normally would have shown little interest in throwing fruit pies to the floor, and who, if he were carrying more than two books, usually managed to drop one of them, now seemed possessed of a demonic fury. His eyes stared in his head, and his hand trembled.

The dish twisted over between them and dumped its contents on the floor with a dead damp sound. In the very brief silence that ensued I could have sworn I heard the knocking of the rope against the flagpole on St Colette's Tower on the far side of the Cloisters. Every diner was frozen in amazement at the result of this bizarre struggle. Jenkins looked at the Butler and then at the Principal for help. Perhaps he thought that Speedfall was going to murder him. The Butler also looked at the Principal: these events were beyond his control. The Principal looked at his gavel, as though if he were to say a premature grace everything would somehow be all right. Or perhaps he had thought of taking up the gavel and hitting Speedfall with it. It was one of those moments when you can hardly believe that anything at all will happen next, so suspended was the ordinary course of events, so unexpected the interruption.

As the silent seconds ticked by, someone giggled. Then, with a suddenness and violence equal to the fate of the St Patrick's Mulberry Pie, Speedfall clapped one hand to his neck and rushed from the Hall with a weird cry, and conversation broke out again, excited and speculative.

'Poor man,' said Prettihow on my left. 'It's the celibacy that does it. The human frame can withstand a surprising amount of quite severe philosophy (and I can believe that there are extensive tests that have proved it) but with additional celibacy you simply don't stand a chance.'

I didn't really feel that it was a matter for joking, and when it became clear that the Principal was more concerned with obtaining another Mulberry Pie from the kitchen that with doing anything about poor Speedfall, I became quite cross and left the Hall myself to see how he was. I didn't need to look for him: he was in the Smoking Room, where we repair after dinner, sitting in a far corner, clutching something on his knees and staring into space.

'How are you feeling, old chap?' I asked. 'What's up?'

I suppose I was expecting some sort of confession or breakdown, and the prospect of spending the rest of the evening coping with Speedfall's private life or with emotional anguish of any kind when I had intended to see the new Herzog film, did not vastly appeal to me.

'Quick, give me your handkerchief,' he said. 'Mine's not big enough.'

Not big enough for what, I wondered. Not tears, surely? Far from being tearful, Speedfall seemed relatively calm, even quietly triumphant, as though his latest performance had achieved some mysterious and indirect aim that we would all discover soon enough. The object on his knees proved to be the Smoking Room tobacco jar. He took my offered handkerchief and, while somehow managing to keep the jar firmly between his lap and elbow, tied one corner of it to a corner of his own. Then he tied both linked handkerchiefs around the jar, looping them about the knob of the lid so that the lid was held firmly in place and the knotted ends of the handkerchiefs sticking up like rabbit's ears. He smiled, and suddenly seemed quite ridiculous sitting there with a thing on his lap that looked like nothing so much as a cartoonist's notion of a bad toothache. Then his smile faded and his anguish returned.

'But what am I going to do with it now?' he asked.

'What do you mean, do with it? What is it? What's the matter?'

I thought that if I could bring him a coffee, calm him down and put the tobacco jar back on its shelf I might be able, if not to fathom the mystery of his strange behaviour, at least to leave him with a clear conscience. The others would eventually finish dinner, and he would not be left alone for very long. He was welcome to my handkerchief, if it made him happy.

He leaned forward, clutching the jar, and whispered solemnly:

'It's terrible. You'll hardly believe it. But I've caught it at last. It's a ghost.'

He seemed perfectly serious, so of course I had to stay and hear all about it. Clutching the tobacco jar, he began to tell me.

'I don't know how much you know about young Maggs? Who worked in the kitchen? Probably nothing at all, I suppose. I thought so. We don't know about these things, do we? I knew about him because I was on the Domestic Services Committee at the time of his appointment and I do take an interest in its business. Someone has to, haven't they? You know how hopeless the Bursar is. I rather pride myself on the attention I pay to details. It's the details that are going to matter in the long run.

'The Bursar loves to steamroller all the business through the DSC so that he can get away for a game of golf before the Mitre opens. There are two ways you can do that, aren't there? You can either explain everything in great detail, lots of boring bumf, so that the Committee feels that it must be all right and just rubber-stamps it. Or you can keep it mysterious and put almost nothing on paper, so that the Committee is totally in the dark about most of the items and is forced to agree to them simply out of ignorance. The Bursar chooses the second way, and I don't like it. And what's more, I make sure that he knows that I don't.

'We were all looking at our watches on the day that we were asked (among a hundred and one other things) to approve the appointment of Kenneth Maggs as second under-chef at eighty-nine pounds a week, and like most such items it would probably have gone through on the nod if I hadn't spoken up. Was this Kenneth Maggs by any chance a relation of "Dog's Nose" Maggs? If he was, wasn't it likely that his skills in the kitchen were as minimal as those of "Dog's Nose" as groundsman? Did he in fact have any skills at all? Shouldn't we have an interviewing committee to look at the colour of his nose and discover whether or not he also was addicted to that revolting collocation of beer and gin which gave rise to his uncle's nickname? Yes, it did turn out that this was nepotism of the most flagrant kind. The Bursar was conniving at it in the most shameless way, since the lad had no qualifications at all.

'I made sure that the decision was postponed and that we advertised the job. The Bursar objected that it ought to be within his own discretion to hire and fire such minor College staff, but the only by-law we could find had of course been completely outdated by inflation, and in any case, as I argued, why had the item come before the Committee at all if we were not to consider it carefully?

'It was a good thing that we did, because he was absolutely hopeless. As a matter of fact he was little more than a football hooligan. I expect you're wondering why he eventually got the job, then? No one else applied! I couldn't understand it. I expect it was all fiddled by the Bursar, but to what end I never discovered. Maggs sat there sullenly while the Bursar beamed all over him and actually apologised to him for calling him back for an interview. He even went so far as to indicate that it was my doing: "Dr Speedfall has usefully pointed out that we have not proceeded quite correctly in this matter" or some such nonsense. That wasn't it, was it? It wasn't simply the procedure; the job should have been advertised in the first place. But it made it look as though I was his enemy, and Maggs kept on glowering at me after that. Have you even seen anyone looking smug and glowering at the same time? It produces a very horrible expression, I can tell you.

'I should have been warned then, I suppose. If we were going to appoint this layabout as a kitchen scullion despite all opposition, as I could see we were, then I ought to have kept quiet. There are many more important things to worry about. But I didn't keep quiet. I was annoyed.

'Perhaps you remember me complaining about the things that went wrong? Dirty vegetables at lunch, over-cooked rice, those impossible dumplings? Oh God, those dumplings. You do remember them, don't you? Some of our colleagues will eat anything. But even Campling spoke when he tried to cut into his dumplings. It didn't take me long to trace it all to Maggs.

'The chef wasn't keen on Maggs either and was quite ready to keep him up to the mark. It seemed to me that I was calling in at the kitchen two or three times a week with some complaint or other. If it wasn't the food it was something else. I once found him playing football in the Cloisters, and made the chef be very strict about his time off. What a mistake! How could I have done it? I ought to have taken warning from the way Maggs looked at me. It had developed from a glower to a glare. He had a weasely sort of face that could look positively malevolent on a dark evening if you came upon him unexpectedly. It often seemed to me that when I happened to pass the kitchen he would be there staring at me from behind the misty glass like a gargoyle, sharpening a long knife.

'One day I had a visit from the groundsman. I couldn't think at first why he should want to see me, but it was soon clear that he had come about "poor young Ken" as he kept calling him. Old Dog's Nose isn't the most articulate of men, is he? I couldn't get a plain proposition from him. He just went on about being fair. Were we being fair to young Ken? Did I know about his poor Mum? Well, I didn't know anything about his poor Mum and I didn't want to, either. Dog's Nose insisted on telling me, though. He sat there holding his cap in both hands as though he was about to push it into my chest, his eyes wandering about my room as if I might have a pint of Dog's Nose hidden in it some-where.

'He then went on to tell me that the boy was deeply into the occult. He made it sound a very solemn business indeed, and I suppose he thought it might impress me with evidence of his abilities. It had begun, as it usually does, with Dennis Wheatley novels from the local news-agents, had progressed through ouija and table-rapping and now he was a member of some sort of coven in Cowley. I said that I wasn't much interested in his second-sight; what I was interested in was his ability to make a mayonnaise. Actually, I wasn't sure that he had much of either. I had been thinking for some time that we ought to require all our College staff to have the proper qualifications, and if neces-sary to acquire them on the job by taking the appropriate evening course at the Polytechnic. I said as much to Dog's Nose, and he turned a shade of pale green, about the colour of one of his own insufficiently-watered cricket pitches. I'd never seen such a baleful look on anyone, least of all some-one who had come to me more or less cap in hand on behalf of a feckless relative about whom little good could be said. He seemed quite agitated, and he intimated that no good would come of crossing young Kenneth in such a matter; certainly no good would come to me and probably quite a lot of harm in fact. He gave me the impression that my wax figure would be stuck with pins and that my life wouldn't be worth living.

'Yes, I know what you're going to say. I can see it in your face. Why didn't I leave well alone? Why did I bother? Well, for one thing I didn't believe him, of course. I didn't really take much account of what he was saying. And then, I don't like being put off something that I'm determined to do if I think that it's right to do it. The very next time I saw that malevolent weasel's face staring at me from the glass window in the door to the kitchen, staring at me because he wasn't concentrating properly on the job, *couldn't* concentrate because he didn't know how to do the job in the first place, I determined to get the DSC to agree to the scheme I mentioned. It wasn't only young Maggs who was involved, I should say, but once the decision had been through the Governing Body it meant that he and one or two others were required to pass their City and Guilds before the year was out. Naturally I felt I was doing the College a service. I was doing the Bursar's job for him. I didn't (I swear it) simply have it in for young Maggs. Though as it turns out he certainly had it in for me.

'The chef says that when Maggs heard that he had to go to evening classes and that it was all my doing he became quite impossible. He had always been awkward and idle, but now he was moody and unreliable and even violent. Dishes he merely cracked before now smashed to smithereens; already butchered meat was further butchered; macedoines were macerated. I expect it was me he was thinking of as he wielded his chopper. I can't think what prevented him ascending my staircase with it one dark night and finishing me off there and then. I suggested to the chef that we could dismiss him if he wasn't doing his job properly, but the chef seemed to think that it wasn't as easy as all that. I then suggested that the chef had a word with Uncle Dog's Nose, but it turned out that Uncle Dog's Nose was mysteriously laid low with arthritis. I thought momentarily of pins stuck in wax, but like you I didn't think I was superstitious and put the thought from my mind.

'The food went from bad to worse: limp toast and chalky

eggs for breakfast, burst sausages for lunch. I could have
sworn that one salad we were given had been mistakenly
made up with carrot peelings. One evening on High Table
when we had medallions of pork in cream with prunes (a
dish of which I am particularly fond) the cream was very
dubious, the prunes were unstoned, and I actually found a
piece of pig's tail in mine. I had to leave the bones on the
side of my plate. It was quite ridiculous. You could hardly
dare to bring a guest to dine any more. It was too shaming.
When Jason Fondling came over from King's to conduct
his symposium on *The Symposium*, I had to take him out to
the Sorbonne to get a decent meal. You may not have
noticed, since you don't dine in all that often.

'I didn't see why Maggs should have such an effect on
the kitchen's performance. I suppose it was just totally
demoralising, a case of the one rotten apple going through
the whole barrel. Unless it was some sort of black magic.
Do you think he could hypnotise the chef, turn the milk
sour, that sort of thing?

'Then suddenly one evening I actually enjoyed dinner. It
was an extraordinary experience. Everything was correctly
cooked. I'd quite forgotten what it was like. It seemed the
decent thing to do to go and compliment the chef, especially
since I'd been pretty well hounding him about Maggs for
weeks. For once I didn't see that weaselly face skulking
behind the stoves, and the chef himself seemed unusually
relaxed. I found him in his little office eating a chicken leg,
beaming all over his face. Maggs had apparently some days
before gone mildly berserk with his chopper and having
effectively destroyed the raw materials for the High Table
entrée, had then proceeded to destroy his hand. Could it
have been deliberate, in some perverse way? A kind of

accusation? An apportioning of blame? Anyway, his thumb was hanging by a thread. The chef said he was used to accidents in the kitchen, but this one was the worst he'd known. They bundled him up and drove him to the John Radcliffe in something of a panic. You've read of the wonderful things they can do with microsurgery these days, haven't you? The John Radcliffe has notched up one or two sensational cases itself and was fully prepared to sew the thumb back on again. There was only one problem. When they unwrapped the horribly bloody towel from his hand in the Emergency Ward they couldn't find the thumb. They looked for it everywhere. They dashed outside and lifted up the seats in the chef's car. They looked for it in Reception. Not to be found. The chef drove back to College and looked all over the kitchen, but there was nothing. He asked the first under-chef, who was sautéing the pork for that evening's High Table, but he'd seen nothing either.

'The thumb had completely disappeared, and Maggs's hand had to be patched up without it. I was astonished to hear all this, of course, and very sorry for Maggs, though I could hardly believe that it was my fault. Really, he'd brought it on himself, hadn't he?

'There was something else about the chef's story which unnerved me, however. You will guess what it was. It gradually dawned upon me as he spoke that the day on which Maggs had lost his thumb was the day on which that pork and prune dish had been served in Hall. A wave of nausea filled my throat as I suddenly realised with horror that what I had thought was a piece of pig's tail in a dish of pork fillet (a ridiculous idea, which even Jane Grigson could not have countenanced) was, in fact, Maggs's thumb, which I had delicately sucked clean off its bones, leaving them on the side of my plate. Oh God, how disgusting! How incredible! I could hardly tell the chef this. I left the kitchen in a hurry and spent a miserable afternoon wondering what it was like knowing that one was a cannibal, and whether it changed one's character utterly.

'It seemed such a bizarre accident. I mean, what do you think the chances are in the circumstances of Maggs's thumb being served up to *me*, of all people, his persecutor? There must have been a dozen or more dining that night. It seemed uncanny to me, and the more I reflected on the uncanniness of it the more I remembered Dog's Nose's dark warnings about Maggs's occult powers. I found it hard to believe that Maggs could somehow have willed me to eat his thumb, but what I did begin to suspect, incredible as it seemed at first, was that not only had he contrived with deliberation to leave his thumb amongst the cut-up pork for that evening's dinner, but that he had expressly cut it off for that end in the first place. What purpose could be served by it? It made me think of young conscripts shooting off their toes to avoid being sent to the front. What did Maggs want to avoid?

'I don't think he wanted to avoid anything, unless it was having to take his City and Guilds. I think that above all he wanted to challenge *me*. Or let's say that his It wanted to challenge and rebuke me. It was his It wanting to transfer guilt on to me. I don't suppose that he made a conscious decision to chop his own thumb off, do you? I mean, you couldn't, could you?

'I was sickened and horrified, and that ought to have been the end of it. Maggs was quite unfit to return to work, and the College had to pay him some sort of pension to avoid any investigation into the conditions in the kitchen.

The Environmental Health Officer is no friend of ours, as you know. I never expected to see Maggs again, and I certainly never want to: the memory of that weaselly leer is quite enough for me.

'But that was when the whole business really began. That was when it all started happening. I was dining one evening with a guest (the food had actually improved) and we were discussing the constituents of the soup. I'd just been looking at the menu a second before, but hadn't remembered the spelling of the soup, which was of a kind I wasn't particularly familiar with, so I reached for the menu again. I could have sworn it moved away from my grasp; it was now just out of reach. I had to ask Curidge to pass it to me, and when he did so there was a big thumbprint on it; a brown thumbprint, still wet. I didn't like to say anything to Curidge, but I looked carefully at his hands and they seemed perfectly clean and dry to me. He isn't a messy eater.

'I didn't like that thumbprint. It seemed like an evil omen. I tried to think of it as a strange coincidence, but it brought to mind the sallow face of Maggs grinning at me.

'I suppose that brown smudge was a knowing signal to me, boldly planted on the menu card just to the right of the College crest, like a police specimen. What could have put it there? What apparently invisible means other than an actual but invisible thumb?

'The next evening food began to fall off my fork. I would be trying to talk and eat at the same time, as of course one has to without looking boorish, and I'd be in the middle of some scintillating repartee and find myself thrusting a completely empty fork into my mouth. After a while I gave up, and went to bed that evening quite hungry.

'If you remember I showed you it happening one evening.

157

I was trying to pour some salt on to the side of my plate, and the thumb was over the hole, preventing the salt from coming out. Yes, I was convinced by then that it was an invisible thumb, behaving as a thumb might do if it wanted to get up to mischief without being seen. You did see what happened, didn't you? The salt wouldn't come out at all, and the next minute it was all over the place. Well, it was a thumb. Maggs's thumb, of course. The thumb he'd lost. It was somehow haunting me.

'You think that's ridiculous, don't you? I remember you saying that you're not superstitious. Well, I am; or at least, I am now. If you can be haunted by the ghost of a dead person, why can't you be haunted by the ghost of a dead thumb? It's still a ghost, even if it's only a small one. Possibly it's the smallest ghost in the world, and it's capable of doing a good deal of haunting.

'If a night went by without its appearance I was ridiculously relieved. On one occasion (do you remember?) I stood everyone the best port at my own expense. Fatal! The next night it was worse than ever, skimming my wine glass out of my hand and holding my spoon to the table. I tried to catch it, but it always moved quickly somewhere else. It even cockily hooked itself in my snuff pocket as though it wanted to drum its missing fingers on my waistcoat front, and then it flipped out my snuff box on to the floor. I had to crouch down to reach for the box, and the thumb kept moving it out of my reach.

'The thing only appeared in Hall. I suppose if I had ever dared to go near the kitchen again it would have haunted me there, too. There was obviously a natural limit, or rather a supernatural limit, to its sphere of operations. There was also, thank goodness, a physical limit to what it was capable of, not having a finger as well and not therefore being able to grasp or pinch. It tended at first just to move things about, not even so that anyone else would really notice. Then it began to get violent. It had a go at my flies but didn't get very far (you try unzipping yourself with just your thumb) and thrust itself up my nose. Once it had started tackling me at close quarters I could get the occasional feel of it: rough and bony, with a cracked nail. It always managed to wriggle out of my grasp, though.

'You saw what happened tonight, didn't you? It was pressing down on my own thumb to make me spill that pudding. Jenkins resisted, and I couldn't pull my hand away. I was suddenly angry when the dish fell to the floor, and when I felt the thumb reaching for my jugular I managed to catch hold of it and stay holding on to it. I'd never done that before because it is so incredibly wiry and strong and feels so horrible, too: I hadn't wanted to touch it at all. But I did so then because I felt that I had the strength to catch it. And I did. It wriggled like anything, but I held on. The stump still felt damp.

'I had to find somewhere to put it. That's why I ran out of the Hall. The thing seems palpable, though invisible. I mean, it doesn't seem to be the sort of ghost that can pass through solid objects. I held on to it and was therefore able to carry it. I just held it in my hand as it tried to twist away, like a little torso. It was like holding a frightened bird, except that it was a bird without limbs or feathers, a vigorous nude bird contorted and jack-knifing in my palm. I couldn't find anything safe to put it in except the tobacco jar. I expect it's all right with the lid tied down like this. But what shall I do with it now?'

I heard Speedfall's story with a combination of mounting alarm and incredulity. As he launched into his narrative he spoke eagerly, even with animation; but all the time he remained very pale, like a man still suffering from shock, and his voice had a tremulous earnestness and urgency which seemed worlds away from fiction. In any case, Speedfall is the ideal butt of a practical joke and would never, for the world, dream of perpetrating one himself.

I couldn't help thinking again of what we were all up to at St Patrick's, about the platonic idea that was the elusive object of the scholar's quest. Did my truth, Speedfall's, Curidge's, Campling's, Prettihow's and all of us, did this remote notion of what we all ultimately wanted to establish as *the* truth every day, every term, every year, every century, not least at this particular November eight o'clock with the river mists beginning to frost the stone-set mullions of the Smoking Room's gothic windows; did this vague, demanding intellectual duty have any room in it anywhere for the challenging unassimilable presence, the irritating ineffective quotidian reality, that was (as I now forcefully apprehended) represented by Maggs's thumb? My mind felt suddenly sullied by Maggs's thumb. It was a thumb to destroy theorems and paradigms. It was an omnipresent and flexile instrument of academic rape, the hopeful revenge of the dismissed realities. It was, simply, a dangerous and hitherto neglected thing.

'Thank you for being such a loyal friend,' said Speedfall. 'I'd got to the point where I simply couldn't cope any more.'

As he said this, he rose and sighed deeply. Then, with a shrug of trust and helplessness, he put the tobacco jar into my hands and left the Smoking Room.